THE MAGIC
OF
THE LAMP

The Tantalising Tales Collection

Lorelei Johnson

An Aladdin and the Wonderful Lamp Retelling

Cover design by: Lorelei Johnson

Editor: Hailey Nicholls

ISBN: 9798433798182

Prologue

Jafar

J afar ran down the darkened alley, his heart pounding wildly, his muscles burning. He clutched a pouch tightly to his chest, afraid of spilling the precious contents as he fled from the angry shouts behind him. He had to make it home, but he had to lose the guards first.

He ducked down another alley, dodging washing and puddles of filth best not scrutinised too closely. His breaths were ragged as they ripped their way from his lungs, clawing at his throat. He could still hear the heavy footsteps behind him but he didn't dare look back.

He'd been sloppy in his desperation, he'd known it was risky, but he'd had little choice.

A pain suddenly exploded in his chest, the air knocked from his lungs as he was thrown back against the ground with the force of his own momentum. The aching pain barely registered as he sucked in air, the pouch still gripped tightly in his small hands. He saw a shadow of movement out the corner of his eye, a sense of dread settling in as he struggled to catch his breath.

'You're a fast one,' the man sneered as he pressed his foot lightly over Jafar's hand. A warning. 'Hand it over.'

Jafar clutched the pouch tighter to his chest and squeezed his eyes shut as he braced for the guard's promise of violence. The man stepped down, slowly applying more and more pressure. Pain sparked, burning brighter and brighter until he heard the crack of bones. He clenched his teeth together, refusing to make a sound, refusing to give the man the satisfaction of his screams.

More footsteps behind him, pain screaming in his hand, sweat on his brow, cold metal to his throat. He gripped the pouch tighter, knuckles turning white. Someone grabbed the pouch pulling it, and Jafar struggled against the bigger man.

'No!' he screamed, gritting his teeth as he tried to tug it back. His heart stopped at the sound of the fabric tearing. White powder and herbs scattered on the breeze. It had all been for nothing. He'd failed.

The sword left his throat, and the world seemed out of focus, a ringing in his ears blocking out the sounds around him. The first kick connected with his jaw, throwing him back against the dirt. He felt the blood trickling down his face, the blows from the men landing strong again and again. His breath echoed in his ears, pain throbbed, ribs cracked, he could barely hear his own screams.

How long had he lain there in the street shrouded in darkness? How long ago had they left him, just another street rat to live or die by God's grace? He could see the moon was high in the sky with his one good eye, the other was swollen shut. His breaths were laboured as he lay in the dirt trying to regain the feeling in his body. He grunted as he pushed himself to his feet, then spat blood to the ground. It was a miracle he still had all his teeth, though he definitely had a few broken ribs. His mother would worry when she saw him like this.

He shuffled home, as fast as he could manage, hoping that she could wait until tomorrow for her medicine. Tomorrow, he could try again. Provided he could still move.

The lights were off when he got to the house, an unusual sight that made his heart squeeze in his chest. He pushed open the door, peering into the darkness. It was silent save for the throbbing in his ears. 'Mother?' he called out but there was no answer.

He fumbled in the dark for the candle, it took him three tries to light the wick with his trembling hands. The flame sparked to life, throwing a warm orange glow on the room. He paused there for a moment, taking a deep breath before picking up the candle and turning to see what he was so afraid to.

His mother lay in her bed, her skin impossibly pale, her eyes staring unseeing at the ceiling. She was so still, like a statue, her dark hair spilling around her. He crept closer, tears welling in his eyes. She wasn't breathing. If only he'd been smarter, if only he'd been faster, she would still be alive.

He howled with frustration, with grief, throwing the candle to the wall. It cracked, wax flying across the room, flame snuffing out, leaving him once again in darkness. His hands curled into fists, nails biting into flesh, blood sliding down his palms, dripping from his knuckles. He vowed that he would no longer be weak, he would take his power, he would get his vengeance, and none would ever stand in his way again.

Jafar could feel a presence behind him, the smell of jasmine hanging gently on the air. He'd been in the palace for some years now, working diligently until he was accepted as an apprentice to one of the scribes, and finally, he was allowed access to the vast library in the palace. The place that held the key to his success. The place only men were allowed, excepting the maids who cleaned it.

Men did not wear jasmine-scented perfume.

He continued reading his scroll, though it no longer held his full attention. Closer, closer, the scent growing stronger until he could feel breath on the back of his neck. He raised an eyebrow, resisting the urge to smile.

'Haven't you learnt your lesson yet, princess?' he asked, his eyes never leaving the page.

Princess Jasmine was the sultan's only daughter. The queen seemed unable to have any more children and the sultan refused to try with anyone but his beloved wife. Anyone would think the princess would grow up spoilt, entitled, insufferable, but the child had surprised him on many occasions, proving herself to be clever and fierce, with a strong sense of justice. She exhibited qualities that would have been amiable in any prince. Perhaps she was trying to appease her father, perhaps her parents didn't curb these tendencies in her. Whatever the reason, he found her creeping into the library more and more.

'How am I to learn anything useful if I'm not to read anything?' she asked, peeking at the scroll over his shoulder.

Jafar folded the scroll over, hiding the words from her prying eyes and she clicked her tongue in irritation. He turned to look at her then. At ten years old, she was curious, more so than he'd expected from a girl her age, not that he had much experience with children in general. His own childhood had ended well before he'd reached ten years, with his father gone and his mother ill. Sometimes he resented the princess for her happy family, knowing she would never want for anything, but it was strangely difficult to despise her for her good fortune.

'You know they're all frowning at you,' he said, subtly nodding his head to the other men in the room. This was not a place for women, and they did not approve of the princess being in their sacred space.

'Let them frown,' she said confidently, raising her chin in defiance. 'They are only sour that I outrank them.'

The corner of his lips curled the tiniest bit before he reigned in his emotions. She was right, of course, but she was far too young to be so observant of the world around her. Was she really that bright or merely reciting her mother's words? He'd spent very little time in the queen's presence, he had no way of knowing.

'They're all afraid to speak to me, but you're not.'

'There's not much that frightens me, princess. Certainly not little girls sneaking into places they shouldn't be,' he said. He raised his hand and flicked his fingers, shooing her away, but she only frowned at him.

'Please, let me read with you. Just for a bit. No one would have to know,' she said, looking up at him with pleading eyes.

'They'd know, and I'd be thrown out of here quick smart. I've worked too hard to let you be my downfall.'

'They wouldn't say anything, because then they would have to tell my father why *they* didn't put a stop to it.'

'Don't you have cushions to embroider?' he asked, feigning irritation. There was something about her carefree and rebellious nature, her search for knowledge denied to her that made it impossible for him to get frustrated with the girl. She reminded Jafar of himself, though she was far less jaded.

Her frown turned into a scowl. 'You're not a very nice boy, Jafar.'

'I'm not a boy,' he snapped, finally sensing a genuine spark of irritation.

She raised a sceptical eyebrow. 'You're eighteen. That makes you a boy.'

Petulant child. She certainly seemed to know exactly where to poke to get a rise. 'That makes me a man. How do you know how old I am, anyway?'

She looked strangely proud of herself then, as if she'd managed a great feat. No matter how he looked at her, she was a very strange princess. He wondered if she would grow out of it. Her father would certainly hope so, if he was to marry her off one day.

'I have my ways,' she said smugly.

He opened his mouth to retort when a loud bang shook the building, sand falling from the ceiling. It was soon followed by screams and cries, the sound of clanging metal.

The men in the library quickly stood, fear evident on their faces as they hesitated, looking about them, waiting for someone to lead the way. Another loud bang, the walls trembled, the men quickly fled.

'What's going on?' Princess Jasmine asked. This ten-year-old princess was putting on a braver face than the men more than four times her age, but Jafar could see the fear in her eyes, hear the quiver in her voice. The palace was under attack, but for some reason he couldn't bring himself to tell her that. She wouldn't know the reason behind the attack, he supposed, but he had been expecting it for months now, what with the skirmishes on the border, though most of the sultan's advisors didn't think it would actually come to it, and thus most of the men in the palace had laughed the very idea off. They'd clearly spent too long living their comfortable lives behind the safety of their walls.

Figures that he'd be stuck with the child while the other men fled for their lives. He let out a weary sigh. 'No questions,' he said, taking her wrist in his hand and dragging her through the library. He opened one of the secret hatches known only to the scribes which led to a small crawl space, not big enough for a grown man, but plenty big enough for a child to hide. 'Get in.'

She looked at that small space then back at him. 'What about you?'

Stupid princess, worrying about a worthless scribe's assistant. 'I won't fit, now get in before you get me killed.'

She hesitated a moment then nodded. She curled herself into the space and he closed her in. She would be safe there, so long as he lived long enough to tell someone where she was. He fled the library, following the other fleeing residents, the soldiers fighting the invaders, though Jafar couldn't help thinking the number was far too small for a true invasion. It looked more like a suicide mission.

'Find the girl!' someone shouted, slicing his way out of the palace and through the crowd. The colours of their armour meant they were southern, Arinian or Lenesian. He couldn't remember. It didn't matter, he slipped through the crowd, avoiding the men. As he hurried inside the safety of the palace walls, he felt relieved that he'd thought to hide the princess in the library. If he'd fled with her, they'd both be dead.

Chapter 1

Jafar

The palace was abuzz, the commotion a monumental distraction. Everyone from servants to nobility were wagging their tongues over the return of their princess. Princess Jasmine had been away for fifteen years, ever since the invasion and the assassination of her mother. The sultan had grieved his wife fiercely, so fiercely that even Jafar felt pity for the man. Afraid to lose his daughter the same way, and convinced he could not turn her into the princess the kingdom needed, he'd sent her away to be schooled by the matrons.

Jafar wondered if these matrons had managed to tame the wilful girl, to quell that rebellion in her, or had she proved too much for them?

He headed to the throne room, sceptre in hand. It was a gaudy thing, a brilliant gold snake with ruby eyes. His eyes had nearly bugged out of his head when the sultan had presented it to him, though he'd quickly recovered so as not to give anything away. It was obvious the sultan had no idea what it was, but Jafar recognised it instantly from his studies into magical objects. The Sultan had seen it only as a fitting reward for the man who'd save his daughter's life, along with a promotion to advisor's assistant. But Jafar saw much more than that, he saw opportunity.

Of course, the promotion hadn't exactly endeared him to his rivals and superiors. But the sceptre had helped him secure his position as he rose through the ranks, but he used it sparingly. He'd quickly learnt that its magic came with a price. Still, it had also taught him a valuable lesson. He needed power to protect his position, he needed power to keep his enemies at bay. Resting on your laurels got you dead and he was not about to suffer death by complacency.

'The princess returns today,' Iago said, and Jafar barely resisted the urge to roll his eyes. 'Will you be glad to see her again?'

This time, Jafar really did roll his eyes. Iago wasn't the brightest spark, but he was loyal and not afraid to get his hands dirty. He was one of the few people Jafar could count on, and being able to trust Iago was the least Jafar should be able to expect, given that he'd once saved the man's life. But there were times when he tried Jafar's patience.

'What a ridiculous question. What is she to me?' Jafar asked, his voice devoid of any emotion.

In truth, he hadn't thought about the princess much since she'd left. She was a child, an amusing little thing at the time, but certainly nothing to him. He'd had much bigger things to focus on. Though he'd made it to chief advisor now, there were many who sought his downfall, some resorting to assassination attempts, some endeavouring to turn the sultan against him. All had failed. The sultan would not so easily believe the man who'd saved his daughter was a traitor.

And he was not a traitor. That didn't suit his needs at all. Why would he betray the source of his power? He had the sultan's ear, and he had no aspirations to wear the crown himself, not when he could wield power in the shadows and be spared the scrutiny. At thirty-three years of age, he'd achieved what no one else had.

'Oh – well, I thought...' Iago stammered, awkwardly running a meaty hand through his hair.

'Enough. What of the lamp?' Jafar asked, changing the subject.

'If I may, master, you have many magical items now, is this one really so important?' Iago asked, hanging his head in that way he did when he knew he was asking a stupid question but was determined to ask it anyway.

Jafar glared at him, making him shrink back. 'What of the lamp?' he asked again, his patience wearing thin.

'The last attempt to reach it failed, but we will try again,' Iago said, finally speaking sense.

The lamp was incredibly important, though he kept the details of it close to his chest lest someone in his ranks had loose lips after too much drink or tried to take it for themselves. The lamp housed a Djinn, a being of unspeakable power, bound to the owner of the lamp. With that lamp, he would be untouchable.

Of course, power like that wasn't easy to come by, and the lamp remained just out of his reach, in a cave protected by magic. Of the men he'd sent in, none had survived. He supposed he might have had the skill to retrieve the thing himself, but he wasn't willing to risk his life for it. Death would defeat the purpose of the endeavour.

As he approached the throne room, the doors were opened for him by guards who bowed their heads to him. He'd never imagined he would climb this high, at least not so soon in his life. The uniforms that had once beaten him senseless as a boy now bowed to him. There was much satisfaction in that.

The sultan sat on his throne, his ivory clothes trimmed with gold, his beard pristine white against his bronze skin, and he seemed to be barely containing his excitement. Jafar bowed to the sultan before taking his place, standing to the right of the throne.

'It's been fifteen years, Jafar,' the sultan said, his hands clutching the throne a little too tightly.

'Indeed, Your Majesty.'

'How do you suppose she'll look?' he asked, and Jafar thought he saw a flicker of worry in the old man's eyes.

'I'm sure she will look much like her mother,' Jafar said, though really he had no idea how the princess would look. He hadn't spent much time thinking about it. Daughters often looked like their mothers, did they not? At any rate, it was the answer the sultan most wanted to hear.

There was a commotion outside the doors and a man quickly entered. 'Princess Jasmine, Your Majesty,' he announced, stepping out of the way as both doors were opened wide. The sultan leaned forward in his throne and all eyes turned, all sound ceased, as the crowd waited with bated breath.

Jafar resisted the urge to sigh. It was all too dramatic for so early in the morning and he had other things that required his attention. But he contained his emotions, the sultan was excited for this and he would not dare dampen the mood for him.

Princess Jasmine finally stepped into the room wearing the finest dress money could buy. The exquisite blue fabric brought out a golden glow in her skin, and her dark hair was tied back, styled to perfection, decorated with jewels. A face veil covered her mouth and nose, shimmering in the light, emphasising those dark eyes as she knelt on the floor before her father, her gaze never leaving his.

She was perhaps the most beautiful creature Jafar had ever beheld. He never would have imagined that wilful child would grow into this. The sultan seemed incredibly pleased, and how could he not be? With beauty like that, he could easily find a husband for her. He'd have his pick of allies. Never again would Arinia attack them, for they wouldn't stand a chance at victory.

Of course, preparations had already begun for finding the princess a suitor. He wondered how she would take that news.

'Welcome home, daughter,' the sultan said, a smile on his face, tears welling in his eyes. Jafar often wondered what it would be like to be so free with one's emotions. He supposed only the sultan had the power to do so.

'Thank you, father,' Princess Jasmine said, her tone perfectly regal, though Jafar sensed a tightness there. Was it resentment at being sent away or had the matron's managed to thread that entitlement into her with their training?

Her eyes flicked to Jafar and she held his gaze for a moment that seemed to stretch out for an eternity. He was unable to pull his eyes away, or maybe it was curiosity that held them there. What did she see when she looked at him?

If she was surprised, she didn't show it. If she recognised him, she didn't show it.

He was surprised to find that displeased him, but he quickly shook off the feeling when she focused back on the sultan.

'You look so like your mother,' the sultan said with an affectionate smile.

A sadness flickered across her eyes before her mask settled back in place. She was carefully schooling her emotions, her expressions, giving nothing away to anyone. Where was that fiery little thing who'd snuck into the library? Was that what the matrons had taught her? Had they shown her to cover that fire, keep it hidden and do her duty like a good little girl?

He realised he'd missed the conversation between father and daughter in his musings, and as he stared down at her he found himself wishing she would look back at him. His brow furrowed and he dragged his gaze away from her. Was he really going to let himself get derailed by a woman? A wholly unavailable one? No. He was going to get out of that room and find a way to get that damned lamp. That was his primary concern.

'You must be tired after your journey, my dear,' the sultan said. 'Go and rest, and tonight, we feast for your return!'

A cheer went up from the crowd. The princess rose to her feet, inclining her head delicately to her father, the picture of poise and grace. As she turned, her eyes caught Jafar's for only a second, and then she was walking away, her head high, her shoulders back, and a roll to her hips that caught the eye of every man in the room.

It seemed that he had been right about one thing. She was going to be trouble.

Chapter 2

Jasmine

The palace had changed in her absence. The destruction of the invasion had been repaired, new construction had been undertaken, and where once this was home to her, she now felt like a stranger to this place. Her handmaid led her down corridors as her mind wandered.

Her father had grown old in the past fifteen years. His beard had turned white as the clouds on a sunny day, wrinkles had settled around his eyes, and his waistline had expanded some, though she knew better than to say anything about it to him. She doubted anyone else had, either.

The most surprising change, though, had been to see Jafar standing as her father's right hand. He wore black robes, red trimmed, much finer than the clothes he used to wear. He stood tall and proud, his head high, his black hair falling down to his shoulders, stubble running along his jaw. But his eyes had changed the most, dark and fierce. The years had clearly been both kind and cruel to him, which wasn't hard to imagine. She was sure that no one had ever achieved the position of chief advisor so young. Many would envy him his success.

She barely recognised the man who had saved her life all those years ago, the boy who had left his scrolls out for her to read after he left the library late at night. Something he'd been chastised for more than once, though she doubted anyone knew the reason for his 'carelessness'.

'Here we are, Princess,' her handmaid, Lina, said with a smile as she opened the door. The guards who had been following her took their place on either side of the doorway.

'Is this really necessary?' Jasmine asked them.

'Sultan's orders, princess,' one of them said, an apologetic look on his face. Of course, he had no choice but to do as he was told. Jasmine nodded and stepped inside, grateful for the click of the door behind her, shutting out the outside world.

She looked around her room but recognised none of it. Any trace of her childhood had been erased, before her was the room of a woman, only she'd had no hand in picking anything out. She opened the wardrobe to find it full of dresses and shoes, most of which she didn't recognise. There were drawers filled with jewellery, only made with the finest gems. One caught her eye, a brilliant ruby hanging from a golden chain. Simple in its design and it would go with almost none of her clothes, but the chain was long enough that she could hide it beneath the fabric. She quickly clasped it around her neck.

'You don't usually wear rubies,' Lina said as she inspected the necklace.

'It was my mother's. She never took it off,' Jasmine explained, then she tucked it beneath her dress and closed the drawer again.

'Is it very different?' Lina asked, her eyes trained on Jasmine's face.

One of the things Jasmine liked about Lina was that she was not a stickler for decorum as most others were. It was one of the reasons she'd chosen Lina when she'd been forced to pick from a long line of young ladies presented for the opportunity. The other reason she'd chosen Lina was because the matrons liked her the least. That immediately endeared the girl to her.

She knew better than anyone that palace life was lonely, what she wanted more than a servant was a friend.

'Yes,' Jasmine said and let out a sigh, feeling lost in her own home. It wasn't just the palace that had changed. Her father had changed, his years showing on him, his past stealing the happiness that she used to see so readily on his face.

It seemed the last fifteen years had changed everyone.

Her mind drifted back to Jafar. Now chief advisor, standing beside her father, he looked almost unrecognisable. Stubble where once there had been smooth skin, broad shoulders and a silent strength where once there was a skinny boy of eighteen. She smiled as she remembered him telling her, *I'm eighteen. That makes me a man.*

Was there anything of the boy she had known in there?

She headed out to the balcony, the sun beaming down on her and she looked out over the city below. Agrabah had always been a mystery to her, couped up in the palace for her own safety as a child, then sent away to a different cage entirely after her mother's death.

But sending her away had done nothing to change her ideals, and now that she had returned, she was under no misguided notions. She was back to be married off to some prince or noble, and that man would rule *her* kingdom while she sat at his side, smiling and looking beautiful.

That was not how she envisioned her life and she would not make it easy for her father. She would study, she would learn the city and its people, and she would show her father that she was capable of ruling in his stead when the time came. And when she was ready, she would choose her own husband, someone who could rule at her side rather than over her.

A knock at her door dragged her from her thoughts. She wondered who would be visiting her so soon after her return. She had left no friends behind, no doting relatives besides her father. She turned, leaning her back against the railing so she could see who it was as Lina opened the door.

Lina inclined her head respectfully. 'Jafar, what a surprise,' she said, curiosity clear in her voice.

'I'd like a word with the princess,' he said stiffly.

Lina cast her eyes at Jasmine, a question there. How intriguing. Jafar had come to speak with her. It was out of character. The boy she'd known always treated her as a pest, though he'd still been surprisingly kind. He surely wasn't visiting her for old time's sake. She nodded and Lina stepped aside, opening the door wide for Jafar to enter.

When he stepped into her room, she was able to look at him better. He'd grown taller, there was a strong set to his jaw, a hardness in his dark eyes. He'd always been ambitious, she wondered what he aspired to now that he had reached the highest position in the palace. Had he found a wife? Something dark stirred in her chest at the thought of a beautiful woman waiting for him at home each night.

Strange.

She turned back to the city below, pushing those thoughts from her mind as she waited for him to join her. When she heard his footsteps on the stone floor, she asked, 'Have you come to scold me, Jafar?'

'Have you done something I should be scolding you for?' he countered. He stood beside her, though she could feel his eyes on her, knew he wasn't looking out at the city as she was.

What did he see when he looked at her?

'I assume you know why your father called you back here,' he said, instantly souring her mood.

'Oh yes, he wants to find a husband for his pretty daughter, to hang her like a trophy on some man's shelf,' she said bitterly. 'Have you come to make sure I acquiesce?' She turned to him then, readying the charm the matrons had forced onto their unruly charge. With pouting lips she said, 'And here I thought you'd come to see an old friend.'

She knew Jafar had never considered them friends. She was a child princess, both above and beneath him. But there was a time when she thought of him thus, he was the closest thing she'd ever had to a friend.

A dark look crossed his face. 'I see the matrons taught you well.'

She shrugged. 'I decided to keep the skills that benefited me and ignore the ones that didn't.'

'Still can't embroider, then?' he asked, his lips curling into a smile before he shook it away, as if he hadn't been expecting that reaction from himself.

It was a reaction that had her heart racing. She tried to brush it off, it was merely the excitement of the day, the nerves for the challenge ahead, and seeing her old friend again, grown and intent on denying their past.

'What use would such a skill be when I have a kingdom to run?' she asked brightly. She wanted him to be confused, she wanted him to be unsure if she was telling the truth or merely teasing.

He wanted to assess her, to see how difficult she was going to make this. But she would make the assessment itself difficult. No doubt he, like every other man, would underestimate her because she was a woman. Good. That's how she wanted it. They would never know what hit them.

'So you don't intend to take a husband?' he asked flatly.

'I *intend* to take this process very seriously,' she said honestly. She would do as her father bid, for she had little choice, but she would ensure that *if* she chose one of these pompous princes, that he would be right for her and for the kingdom. Though she suspected that none would measure up. She was far more capable than any of them. How many of them had stayed up through the night, reading the histories and the laws, the treaties with neighbouring kingdoms. How many had researched great rulers, past and present, to garner ideas to make Agrabah better for the future? How many of them could love her country and her people as she did?

Jafar studied her, though if he came to a conclusion, he didn't say what it was. She wanted to know what he was thinking, what he thought of her. But she had more pressing concerns at present.

'If your interrogation is finished, I do have to spend a great many hours at my looking glass to ensure I am the prettiest trophy at the feast this evening,' she said.

'It would please your father a great deal if you would cooperate with him in this,' Jafar said, choosing his words carefully. 'He has been working diligently to make this happen.'

Jasmine paused for a moment. 'How has he been?' she asked, unable to help the note of uncertainty in her voice. She had received letters from him over the years, though they were few and far between. Fifteen years was a long time, he was almost a stranger to her now, but still that love was there for him.

'He has missed you a great deal,' Jafar answered, his eyes softening. He bowed his head to her before leaving her alone with her thoughts once more. Thoughts she didn't have time for because she had a feast to prepare for, one that she was not looking forward to in the slightest.

Chapter 3

Jasmine

Jasmine had allowed Lina to do as she wished that night, styling her hair, adding kohl in a dramatic fashion that drew attention to her eyes, adding colour to her lips, all things that Jasmine had learned the importance of from the matrons. This was her war paint, meant to please and attract, but Jasmine would also use it to distract, not that she would need it. Men had a way of underestimating women, that was a lesson she'd learnt from her mother.

The dress Lina chose was crimson, trimmed with gold, a dark sheer fabric running from her bodice to her skirt, giving all a shrouded view of her torso that bordered on risqué but was still within acceptable parameters. Her ruby necklace sat proudly on her chest, giving her courage, as if her mother's strength were contained within the stone. She had no doubt there would be suitors in attendance that night, and she intended to show them she was more than they could handle.

Lina smiled as she checked Jasmine over. 'They are not going to know what hit them, princess.'

'Good,' Jasmine said, ignoring the flutter of nerves in her stomach. She was relieved Lina would be there, even if she would be standing to the side or serving her. Her presence would be comforting nonetheless. 'Let's go.'

Lina nodded and led her through the palace, already more accustomed to the layout than she was. Once, she'd known every inch of the place, but that felt like a lifetime ago now. She pushed the depressing thought away and focused on keeping her expression neutral. She couldn't let her defences fall tonight.

She could hear the commotion long before she reached the doors to the garden, could smell the roasting meats, the cacophony of perfumes, the jingling of dancer's costumes and beautiful dresses, the screeches of exotic animals, the smell of incense. Her father had spared no expense tonight.

That nervous flutter returned as the doorway loomed before her. She rolled her shoulders back, held her head high. Lina handed her a face veil but she declined it. Though it could offer her a modicum of confidence she didn't feel, tonight they would see her in full, tonight she would show them she would not simper to any man.

She took a deep breath and walked through the doors, the smoke from incense swirling around her, the heat of the night hanging in the air. Dancers on stage twirled around on bare feet, anklets sparkling in the firelight. Brightly coloured fruits stacked in overfilled bowls, beautiful plants, and the gold glinting off the palace décor made the entire scene feel almost surreal, like something out of a children's story. She used to love these parties, but this one had an oppressive air to it as she strode towards the head of the table where her father sat. To his right, Jafar sat tall and proud, his sceptre within reach. She had noted it in the throne room, too. Perhaps it was something he carried around like a badge of office, but there was something about it that unnerved her.

'Ah! The princess has finally arrived,' her father said merrily, already clearly in his cups. 'Fashionably late, my dear. You really put in some effort tonight, that's very good,' he said only for her ears, though she suspected that Jafar hadn't missed a word.

'It has been a long time since I've been home, Baba,' she said as she took her seat, switching to a more endearing term now that she was not before an assembly. A warm smile spread across his face. 'I was a little nervous.'

Jafar raised an eyebrow but settled it quickly. He didn't believe her. But it didn't matter, because her father believed her. 'No need for that, Jasmine. You are the most beautiful woman here. And I have invited many esteemed guests.'

Jasmine barely flicked her eyes at the table. She'd seen them all as she'd entered the room, princes form neighbouring kingdoms who were as yet unwed, a few high-ranking lords who had enough money and connections to make a suitable match. She had been prepared for this, and yet she hadn't expected there to be quite so many of them in attendance.

'And here I thought you'd arranged all this for me,' she said, pouting gently. 'Shame on you, Baba, using this as an opportunity for political manoeuvring.'

The sultan laughed heartily. 'Do you see how clever she is, Jafar? I dare say she would make any man a formidable wife.'

'Indeed, Your Majesty,' Jafar said. She suspected that was his usual response when he wished not to comment on a subject.

'This is a party, and you are young. You should be dancing!' the sultan exclaimed.

As if they'd been waiting for the sultan to make such an announcement, she saw men fidgeting in their seats, eagerly watching, waiting to pounce on her, to claim her first dance and perhaps her heart, though she knew they cared not for love, merely the throne and the power of the sultan. She was a bonus, like a brilliant golden bracelet to hang on their arm, ornamental and only for their own personal enjoyment.

'If you wish to see me dance, Baba, then I shall,' Jasmine announced, smiling warmly at her father even as she was cringing inside. But she need not play their little game, she would much rather play her own.

She rose from her seat and walked around her father's chair, stopping in front of Jafar. He looked up at her with suspicion, not exactly the reaction she'd expected but it would suffice. 'Will you not dance with me, Jafar?'

Jafar seemed lost. It was the first time she'd even seen him unsure of himself and she found it amusing, though she kept her amusement to herself as best she could. Jafar looked over at the sultan who waved him away happily, already starting on his next piece of lamb. She knew he wouldn't dare refuse her, as it would be a great insult to the sultan if he did.

With barely concealed irritation, Jafar stood and took Jasmine's hand, leading her to the dance floor as the whispers of those attending swirled around them. 'Are you looking to start a scandal, princess?' he asked when they were out of earshot.

'A scandal? Why, I'm merely dancing with an old friend,' she said innocently.

He raised his eyebrow at her. 'You didn't take to the matrons' teachings, then,' he said, a statement rather than a question as they traded positions on the floor, turning around each other but always remaining at a distance. This was Jasmine's favourite dance, though she'd never told anyone.

'How do you know what they taught me?' she asked, challenging him. The music moved her body, and her hips rolled tantalisingly as she slowly closed the distance between them.

'You know your father did not intend for you to dance with me. There are many men here tonight he wants you to acquaint yourself with,' Jafar said, changing the subject.

'You haven't changed at all, still as stiff as ever,' she said, turning her back to him, rocking her hips as his hand slid around her waist, the heat of his touch slipping through the sheer fabric there, sending a thrill through her body.

'And you as untameable as ever,' he answered, his voice neutral. Nothing seemed to faze him. She found herself wanting to ruffle that perfectly still surface of his, elicit some reaction from him, some genuine emotion. 'Why did you choose to dance with me?'

She spun around in his arms and he dipped her before spinning her and pulling her close again. He was merely following the steps of the dance, playing the role required of him. Something about that left a bitter taste in her mouth. 'Because you're the only man here who doesn't want anything from me,' she answered honestly.

'Ah, so you wish to correct that, do you? You want all the men in the room to be in love with you?' he asked darkly.

She glared up at him, then spun away. Rolling her hips sensually to the music, she held one arm out, curling her finger at him, a look of sheer confidence on her face. When he was once again close enough to speak to, she said, 'You're still an arse, I see.'

His eyes widened in surprise, not enough to notice unless you were looking for it. 'I'm surprised that a princess would use such language,' he said, tsking at her behaviour.

'Are you? I thought you said I was untameable,' she countered. He spun her a final time, pulling her against him as the music came to an end.

Over the roar of applause, he pressed his lips to her ear and said, 'That brings us to the end, princess.' She could feel his breath warm on her neck and she shivered against it. Before she could say anything more, he released her, taking her hand to escort her back to the table. When he released her hand, she took her seat next to her father, determined not to look at Jafar again for the rest of the night.

Chapter 4

Jafar

The morning light filtered into the room, stirring Jafar from sleep with a groan. His head pounded as he cracked open an eye, the night flooding through his mind as if he'd asked for a replay. He'd drunk far too much wine at the feast, an unusual move for him. He was usually so careful, he needed to keep his wits about him at all times.

But last night he'd let his guard down.

Princess Jasmine had entered the gardens like a siren from legend, tempting men to their destruction. Tempting him to his destruction. The blood had deserted his brain to travel further south, he was unable to tear his gaze from her. The crimson of her dress was fierce and regal, the flash of golden flesh beneath thin fabric drew the lustful eyes of the men who were present for the sole purpose of making her theirs. and yet she had singled him out of the crowd.

Which satisfied him to a troubling degree.

He had no misguided notions on her attentions. She had singled him out because he was a familiar face, perhaps, because of his appearance of disinterest, most certainly. She'd told him as much, and he'd lashed out at her for it like a petulant child. He hadn't realised he'd wanted a different answer from her until his sharp tongue had dealt its blow.

But it was for the best. He hadn't prepared himself for her, but he needed to get over this. Whatever this was. She was not for him, and he had no desire to be sultan. He needed to focus on the lamp.

He pulled himself out of bed and splashed water on his face. His breakfast sat on his desk untouched, no doubt Iago had brought it in and decided not to disturb his sleep. A healthy choice. It seemed the man was capable of learning. But the sun was already high in the sky, he had to hurry. There were many presentations today, the sultan was determined to marry the princess off as soon as possible, for the sake of the kingdom and for her safety.

Of course, he had put the idea in the sultan's head. It was, by far, the best strategy they had of securing the kingdom and fending off any future plans for invasion. There were many rumours of the Arinian army's movements. He was sure they would make a play soon, though his spies couldn't gain any useful information. Whatever their plans, the commanders were keeping them close to their chests.

He pulled on his clothes and grabbed his sceptre just as a clumsy knock sounded on the door. 'Yes?' he said half-heartedly. He knew Iago's knock by now.

'Forgive the intrusion, Master,' Iago said.

'What news?' Jafar asked impatiently.

'Another failure,' Iago said. 'We have a few more candidates, though.'

Jafar sighed. Another failure. Each failed attempt increased the risk that others would find out what he was doing. And it meant more time for him to get distracted.

Jasmine's face came to mind again and he shook the image away. Even if he could have her, she wouldn't want him. Much had changed since she'd left the palace, he'd become ruthless and cold, and he *liked* it that way.

'Did you have fun at the feast last night?' Iago asked, as if he couldn't help himself. 'The princess is very beautiful. The whole palace is buzzing with gossip because she chose to dance with you.'

Gossip was the one thing he aimed to avoid, and he'd managed just fine for the last fifteen years. Then she'd shown up and in a single night had disrupted his entire life. 'She chose me to irritate her father, nothing more,' he told Iago, surprised at how that truth stung. 'And I would have been remiss to refuse her, there is nothing more to say.'

He looked at his untouched breakfast and for the first time since he'd arrived at the palace, his stomach grumbled for food. But he was out of time and he couldn't be late. The sultan would be most displeased if he were. Instead, he headed out the door, once again making his way to the throne room, Iago in tow.

'Are you sure?' Iago asked.

It was the first time the man ever questioned Jafar and it made him stop in his tracks, Iago nearly walking into him. He turned his head, his eyes cold and fierce as he looked down at the man who again shrunk before him, his lips tightly shut.

He was done with this topic.

He marched forward, his pace a little too fast, a scowl on his face that he couldn't seem to shake. As he neared the throne room, he took a deep breath, unwrinkling his brow before entering and bowing to the sultan.

The sultan had an excited smile on his face. Jafar wondered how he could be so eager to marry his only daughter off when he had scarcely seen her in fifteen years, but perhaps the man saw it as a way to keep his daughter close. Either way, it worked in Jafar's favour because his primary goal was to keep Agrabah safe. A war would benefit no one.

Still, there was something about this that bothered him, though he couldn't seem to put his finger on it. 'Are you sure it's wise to do this so soon, Your Majesty?' he asked, his voice audible only to the sultan.

'Why? What did she tell you last night?' the sultan asked, a crease in his brow. It seemed the sultan was having misgivings about the situation, too.

Before Jafar could answer, the doors swung open and one of the Lenesian princes entered. There were three of them in total, all vying for Princess Jasmine's hand and the Agrabahan throne, since their own was occupied by their eldest brother.

The prince had short dark hair and a square jaw, with thick burly muscles that pressed against the fabric of his shirt. He was tall, and easily strong enough to protect the princess, but whether he would actually stick around to do so remained to be seen. Jafar supposed it would depend on how desperately in love with her he fell, and he suspected any price was guaranteed to fall in love with her, if only Jasmine would keep her thoughts to herself, which seemed unlikely.

Jafar caught himself smirking and quickly schooled his expression once more. He should be exasperated with her, he needed her to marry one of these fools.

'Prince Jamil, thank you for coming,' the sultan said.

The prince bowed low before him, then looked up with eager eyes. 'Your Majesty, thank you for your gracious welcome,' he said. He was too eager. Eager for a throne of his own, eager to possess such a beautiful woman, no doubt Princess Jasmine rivalled his brother's wife. From what he knew of Prince Jamil, he was ambitious, clumsy, and strove to step out of his brother's shadow. The sultan of Lenese cast a long shadow, and Jafar doubted that even this would help the prince achieve his goal.

'Princess Jasmine will be with us shortly. She has been long away from home, I fear she has not quite found her bearings.'

The prince nodded in understanding. 'It must be a great comfort for her to be back home again.'

Jafar resisted the urge to roll his eyes. Where was the princess? She needed to come and put a swift end to this. Prince Jamil was not the sultan Agrabah needed, he could tell from a glance that the indulgent oaf would run the kingdom into the ground.

The doors finally opened and the princess entered, a fierce expression on her face. She'd opted for less revealing clothing today, but the outfit clung to her torso, showing her shape and portraying a feminine strength, the kind one might expect of a queen. Despite being a good foot shorter than the oafish prince, she commanded a presence that far diminished him.

She bowed before her father, this time standing right away, rather than staying low before him. 'Good morning, father,' she said formally. Jafar noted the disappointment in the sultan's face, he'd so enjoyed her calling him *Baba* at the feast. Jafar looked at Princess Jasmine with renewed interest. What a calculating woman she had become.

'Jasmine, dear, you remember Prince Jamil from the feast last night?' the sultan said, recovering his composure.

'Yes, Prince Jamil,' she said, inclining her head to him, which baffled the oafish prince. She was treating him as an equal rather than her superior, which was expected of a woman.

'Uh...ah...' the prince stammered before finally regaining his composure. 'Princess, it is good to see you again. I fear I didn't have the opportunity to dance with you at the feast last night.'

He hadn't, but many other contenders had, and each time a man took her to the dancefloor Jafar's glass had filled again. The dull ache in his head stood as a reminder.

'No, how unfortunate,' Princess Jasmine said, though there was little sincerity in her words. 'Tell me, Prince Jamil, why is it that you wish to marry me?'

A gasp was heard on the other side of the room and the sultan frowned while the prince gaped, his mouth flopping open and closed again like a fish. It was all Jafar could do not to burst into laughter, but he managed to hold his composure.

'W-well, aside from the obvious political reasons...' he stammered.

'Yes, aside from those,' she said with a patronising tone.

'Jasmine,' her father warned, but she seemed undeterred and the oafish prince continued to squirm under her gaze.

The prince looked to the sultan then back at the princess but it was clear the meeting had come to an end. 'I apologise, Prince Jamil. We will pick this up again another day, my daughter doesn't quite seem herself today,' the sultan said.

Prince Jamil seemed happy for the excuse to escape. He bowed and fled the room, leaving behind a very smug looking princess. As soon as the prince had left, the sultan's composure began to slip. 'Everyone, please leave us. I must speak with my daughter.'

It had been a long time since Jafar had seen the sultan lose his temper. The princess had been back not even two days and she had pushed her father to anger. Jafar took a step to leave with the others but the sultan bid him stay with a gesture of his hand.

When the last prying eyes had left, the sultan stood, his face reddening. 'What do you think you're doing?' he demanded.

'Me?' Jasmine asked incredulously. 'You sent me away for fifteen years, and only summon me back to marry me off to some stranger, whose only qualification for ruling this kingdom over me is what's between his legs.'

The sultan and Jafar both stared at her dumbfounded for a moment, as if neither of them could believe what had just come out of her mouth. Her father blustered, but Jafar couldn't help feeling impressed, though perhaps he ought not to.

'Baba,' she said, her voice softening as she switched to that endearment her father liked so much. She hurried towards him, taking his hand in both of hers. 'Baba, please. We don't need to rush this. Let me learn, so I can take your place myself. Who better than I who you raised to love this country and its people? Then there will be no need to rush a marriage. Give me the chance to find the love you and mama had.'

'I cannot. No woman has ever ruled Agrabah before, Jasmine. The other kingdoms would see it as weakness and come to destroy it or take it from you. We need the strength of an alliance through your marriage. Choose well from among those here now, love will come in time.'

She snatched her hands back, tears beginning to well in her eyes, though she turned her back quickly to hide them. She strode from the room, ignoring her father's calls for her.

'Let her be, Your Majesty. I'm sure she merely needs time to come to terms with her responsibility,' Jafar said, sympathy in his voice, though he couldn't tell if it was for the sultan or for the princess.

The sultan let out a sigh. 'You're right, as usual, Jafar. She has her mother's spirit. I should have known it would not be so simple.'

'Perhaps if you explained to her the reason for her need to marry, give her all the facts. She would do what she thought best for her people,' Jafar offered.

The sultan looked at him then, as if he were appraising him. 'You think very highly of the princess.'

'I'm merely stating what I have observed since her return, Your Majesty.'

The sultan nodded. 'I'm sure you have much to attend to, I've kept you quite long enough.'

Jafar bowed to the sultan and happily left his side. He did have much to attend to, including finding someone who could retrieve the lamp from that blasted cave, since Iago seemed incapable. He let out a sigh as he headed to his quarters. It seemed that if he wanted something done right, he would have to do it himself.

Chapter 5

Aladdin

The Agrabah market was a hive of activity; brightly coloured cloth fluttered in the warm breeze, the smell of spices and incense swirled around the gathering customers, jewellery glinted in the morning sunlight. Anything anyone could want could be found in that market place, provided they had the money for it.

Unfortunately, Aladdin didn't. But he'd lived in Agrabah his whole life and managed to make do. His skills had been refined over the years, despite his father berating him to learn a trade. Thieving was a kind of trade, he supposed, and he never had any grand ambitions. He took what he needed to survive, and he lived a relatively easy life. What more could a young man really want? To slave away in some shop or worse day in and day out? No thank you.

As he wandered the marketplace, the merchants eyeing him suspiciously, his fingers found their way into a pocket or two, relieved a woman of a rather beautiful necklace that didn't suit her at all, so really, he was only doing a public service. With his spoils in hand, he made his way to the pawnbroker, a rather severe looking woman who could just as easily pass for a man if she chose to.

'Good morning, Baseema. You're looking lovely today,' he said, filling his voice with as much charm as he could muster.

She rolled her eyes at him and clicked her tongue before holding out her plump hand. Aladdin handed over the necklace and watched as she appraised it with a scrutinising eye. She tossed a small bag of gold at him. 'Now get out.'

'A pleasure as always,' he said with a grin before darting out of the shop. He weighed the bag in his hand then gave a little shrug. It would get him through the next few days.

As he rounded the corner, he stopped in his tracks and blinked hard. A woman the likes of which he had never seen before strolled through the streets, wearing a look of fascination. She covered her head and her mouth with a fabric that he could tell even from a distance was the finest quality, he doubted it was sold even in Agrabah. Her skin was perfect, lightly golden like a wealthy woman's, but her eyes drew him in like none had ever done before.

For the first time in his life, Aladdin wanted something more.

He watched her progress through the market as she looked at every stall, each merchant showing her every kindness -- they could smell money a mile away. Each time she left with nothing, to their immense disappointment.

She stopped suddenly, her eyes looking sad as she beheld a small urchin, clearly starving as most of them were. He was looking at a basket of apples with longing and hadn't noticed the woman yet. She took an apple and handed it to the boy. His eyes went wide and he snatched the fruit with a grateful smile before dashing away. Aladdin had been there;

the boy was afraid that if he stuck around, someone might take it from him.

The merchant began speaking with her, his expression darkening, and Aladdin knew something had gone wrong. He darted forward as the man grabbed her wrist.

'Unhand me this instant,' she demanded with an authority that came with a privileged life. She was used to being obeyed.

'Do you know what we do to thieves around here, missy?' the merchant asked, leering at her with a mouth full of rotting teeth, which elicited a look of disgust from the woman.

'Do you have any idea who I am? If you touch me there will be hell to pay,' she promised, not backing down from the fight, though she clearly had no idea what she was in for.

Aladdin reached them, removing the man's hand from her wrist and placing himself in front of her. 'I apologise, sir. My sister is...a little slow,' he said.

'Sister?' the man sneered, looking from Aladdin's rags to the woman's fine clothes with a disbelieving scowl. 'And are you going to pay for the apple she stole?'

Aladdin had the money to do exactly that, but he wasn't keen to part with it over this, not when he could simply outrun the situation. 'Certainly,' he said, holding up the bag of gold he'd received earlier. He dipped his hand inside then placed a decoy in the man's outstretched hand.

The man snapped his fingers around it without looking, as if he thought Aladdin might try to take it back. He huffed and Aladdin took the woman's hand. She attempted to pull it away but he held tight, leading her slowly away. 'Shh,' he whispered. How far would they get before the man realised he'd been paid with a button?

'Stop! Thief!' the merchant cried, having caught on to the ruse.

Not far enough. 'Run!' Aladdin said, flashing a boyish smile at the woman. He sped up, keeping hold of her hand, leading her through the streets. The guards gave chase, but they didn't know the city like he did.

She kept up surprisingly well, and he couldn't help thinking how soft and small her hand was in his. That combined with her clothes, her posture, her complexion, there was no doubt she was from the palace. But what was she doing out in the city? Very few left the palace, and even fewer women. Everything they needed was there or brought in by servants.

'Up here,' he said, kneeling down so he could boost her up.

She looked at him sceptically but the sound of heavy footsteps soon motivated her. She placed her foot in his hand and he pushed her up. She gripped the ledge and kept climbing. For someone of her status, he was impressed at how capable she seemed as she climbed up the building.

'Stop there!' a guard yelled, bringing him back to his senses. He ran and jumped at the ledge, quickly gaining on his mystery woman. She made it to the roof and he pulled himself up quickly after.

He took her hand again and led her across the rooftops. He knew they wouldn't keep chase too much longer, not over one apple. They came to the last roof and she was breathing heavily. He handed her a wooden pole and she looked at him like he was crazy.

'We have to jump,' he said. She looked down, then back at the pole, tentatively taking it in hand. He heard shouting and he knew the guards were climbing up, too. Damn it. He'd thought they'd give up. 'I'll go first if you –'

Before he could finish his sentence, she had the pole in the ground and was sailing gracefully through the air. She landed on the other side and he blinked at her in surprise, his heart beating a little faster. She stared back at him, a question on her face, and he shook himself. She was no doubt wondering what was taking him so long.

He followed her over and dropped the pole before snatching her hand and leading her over the rooftops. They were quickly out of sight, finally safe, and he knew she was glad they had stopped running. He knew exactly where to take her, too. A rooftop he used as a hideout. It wasn't as fancy as anything she'd be used to but it had a certain charm. It used to be a room, but two of the walls had crumbled away, giving a beautiful view of the setting sun in the evenings, and he'd hung some cloth he'd stolen to decorate the place. Usually he slept there, having no other home to go to, but he wasn't about to tell her that.

'We'll be safe here,' he said. He took a seat and watched as she looked around.

'You live here?' she asked, and that tone in her voice made a deep shame well inside him.

'Nah, it's just a hideout,' he said with a shrug, hoping she couldn't see the red in his ears. He'd never been embarrassed of his lifestyle before, but he knew it wasn't enough to impress this creature before him. He'd never coveted something so fiercely in his life.

Her silence bothered him. He wanted to hear her voice, wanted to know who she was, where she was from. He wanted to keep her here until the moon was high in the sky. Only talking. This time, at least. Would he be able to convince her to meet him again? What would it be like to kiss those supple lips?

He shook himself. He needed to get off that train of thought.

'You're not a very good thief, miss...'

She laughed then, a beautiful and delicate sound, as a woman's laugh should be. 'Miss?' She let out a sad little sigh. 'Jasmine. And I'm not a thief.'

'Jasmine, huh? Like the princess,' Aladdin said, laying on as much charm as he could muster.

She raised an eyebrow at him, an amused little smile visible through the sheer fabric of her veil. He stared at her as if his brain had stopped working. 'No. You're the princess?'

The princess of Agrabah was in his hovel. He had no hope of winning so fine a jewel. Despair began to claw at him. Could he have set his sights higher?

'Sad that my own people don't know me, but I suppose I can't really fault them for that,' she said and she really did seem saddened by it. He hadn't expected her to care so much. He wished she would say something to make him want her less. Then it would be easier to let her go.

'What are you doing in the city?' he blurted out before he could stop himself.

'I wanted to see it,' she said with a shrug. 'Of course, my father would greatly disapprove if he knew I was here.'

'But you came anyway?' Brave princess. If she was his, he would like nothing better than to show her the kingdom, to show her the world. Though he would need money for such things.

'I've been trapped my whole life, never being able to see the world outside my cage. I just wanted to see it, just once.'

He felt like she was holding something back. Just once before what? Of course, he could guess what. It was no secret that the sultan was looking for a husband for his daughter. Aladdin felt sympathy for the princess, even though she was the last person in the world who really deserved his pity. She had everything she could possibly need, not like most of the people in the city. But he supposed in reality, she might just be as powerless as they were, and that was something he could understand.

'And who do I have to thank for my rescue?' she asked, changing the subject.

'Uh, I'm Aladdin.'

If ever he had picked a woman out of his league, this was it. The princess couldn't be further from his reach, and yet, he'd never wanted a woman more than he wanted her. Though, it wasn't as if he could offer her anything. She had the world at her fingertips, and he had nothing.

'Thank you, Aladdin.'

He liked the way his name sounded on her lips and he offered her a smile. What would life be like in her world? If only he'd been born of money, he might be in those meetings the town had been buzzing about, he might be lined up to win her hand with all the other foreign and local dignitaries.

She looked out over the city with an unreadable expression. 'I should go back before my absence is noticed,' she said.

He was reluctant to let her leave, knowing that he would never see her again. But he couldn't exactly keep her. He nodded. 'This way.'

He led her slowly down to the street, wishing he could think of something to say to her, to get her to stay a little longer, to leave a lasting memory of him with her. 'Will I see you again?' he asked, regretting the words as soon as they'd left his mouth. What a ridiculous question to ask.

But she turned and smiled at him, mischief shining in her dark eyes. 'Maybe.'

He watched her walk away, a spark of hope warming his heart. Maybe he would get to see her again. He hoped that he would. Perhaps next time he would have a chance to endear himself to her in some way. He would need to do something about his prospects, though.

For the first time in his life, Aladdin felt that ambition his father had always tried to instil in him.

Chapter 6

Jasmine

J asmine hadn't made it very far before the guards seized her, though not for her accidental thievery. Her absence had been noticed much faster than she'd anticipated, though the guards seemed surprised to find her roaming the streets alone, as if they'd expected she had been kidnapped. They marched her back to the palace, towards the throne room, where her father would no doubt be waiting, along with Jafar.

She supposed for a first escape attempt, it was rather successful, even if she had been caught. Next time, she'd do better.

The man from the market had intrigued her. There was something free about his life that she envied, even though he clearly had very little to his name. He seemed to have a contentment that she had never experienced. She wondered what it would be like to live as he did.

The doors opened and her father glared down at her. He was furious. The last time he'd looked at her like that she'd been nine years old and caught gambling with some of the guards who'd thought her antics were amusing, though they'd been severely reprimanded after. No one would dare look at her after that.

Jafar wore a look of mild disapproval, which bothered her for some reason. Who was he to disapprove of her? She resisted the urge to scowl at him, schooling her expression as the matrons had taught her to do. She bowed before her father, though she did not remain on her knees as she knew she should. Instead, she stood before him, doing her best to radiate strength.

'I don't remember having such a disobedient daughter,' the sultan bellowed.

'Then you and I remember my childhood very differently, Baba,' she said. It was probably true. He had probably forgotten her talent for getting into trouble as the years passed and he hoped that those traits would be schooled out of her by the matrons. But he hadn't counted on one thing; Jasmine *liked* that troublesome part of herself. She wasn't about to let anyone take it from her.

'If it were to get out that you disobeyed me so brazenly, that you are wild, who do you think will marry you then?' he demanded.

'With any luck, all those pompous princes will be disgusted and leave,' she countered, her temper rising. 'You brought me home to bargain me off, trading a princess for an army, my misery for an alliance.'

'It is your duty!' her father roared, spittle flying from his lips, his face so red she thought he might pass out.

'Why? Why can't my duty be to rule? I am just as capable if not more so than any of those spoilt man-children out there.'

'Princess,' Jafar said calmly, stepping forward just enough to draw her attention. He was trying to diffuse the argument that he could no doubt see going nowhere. 'Putting aside your dissuasion to marriage for a moment, can you not see that you put yourself at great risk today? Leaving the palace unattended, un*protected*.'

Her father took a deep breath then, as if remembering why he had summoned her in the first place. 'Jafar is right. It's dangerous out there. What would I do if something happened to you?'

'Nothing happened to me, Baba. I'm fine,' she said. Aladdin's face popped into her head, the run from the guards, she couldn't remember the last time she'd had so much fun. Jafar was scowling and she realised she had a smile on her face. She cleared her throat but found herself unable to meet his gaze.

'That's enough for today. Go and change, we have much to get through.'

And by that, he meant there were more princes waiting to bid for her at the auction. Her smile faded and a sigh escaped her lips. 'Yes, Baba,' she said, knowing that there was nothing more she could say now to change his mind.

She bowed again and left the room, her confidence a little shaken. Was there no way she could get out of this marriage situation? Was there no way she could make her father see her worth?

'Your father was worried about you,' Jafar's voice interrupted her thoughts.

She hesitated a moment in surprise, giving him the chance to catch up to her. He really had changed in her absence. His strong features were strikingly handsome now that he was fully grown. That arrogance had remained, though, which wasn't exactly a deterrent. She shook herself from those thoughts as he looked down at her and continued towards her chambers. 'Yes, he worries a great deal,' she said bitterly.

'Did you see what you wanted to?' he asked, his question surprising her into stopping again. She looked up at him curiously, the intensity in his dark eyes sending a shiver down her spine, reminding her of the dance they shared.

'If I said no, would you offer to show me?' she asked. Why did she so badly want him to say yes?

A smirk curled at the corner of his lips. 'You are so used to having men wrapped around your finger, aren't you?'

He was so close to her and she suddenly felt nervous. She found herself wishing he would reach out with those long fingers and glide them along her jaw, wondering what his skin would feel like on hers. She had to remember herself, she couldn't let him overpower her so easily, as if she were a swooning maid.

'Are you wrapped around my finger, Jafar?' she forced herself to ask, surprised at how confident she sounded as her heart beat wildly in her chest.

'Now where is that charm when you speak to the princes?' he asked, raising an eyebrow.

She felt as if a bucket of cold water had been thrown on her and she glared at him. 'I wouldn't waste my time,' she said stiffly and began walking once more, her pace a little faster than before.

How could she be so easy? Letting a man like Jafar distract her, make her heart race. How naïve could she be?

He was not the sort of man she should attach herself to, anyway.

'Your father only wants your safety and that of the kingdom. Your marriage to a prince is the best way to secure both.'

'Safe and miserable, lovely,' Jasmine muttered, rolling her eyes in disgust.

'There are worse fates.'

'Are there? And which of those are *you* currently experiencing?' she snapped.

'There's that spoilt princess everyone is expecting,' Jafar said darkly.

She turned on him, her temper flaring. 'What do you want, Jafar?'

For a moment she saw something in his face, something that filled her with a curiosity to know his thoughts, a strange sense of expectation sitting on her chest. But instead he said, 'I came to make sure you do your duty.'

She laughed then. 'My own father can't control me, what makes you think you'll fare any better?' she spat. She stormed away from him, slamming the door to her chambers with far too much force to be considered genteel by any measure.

Jasmine had sat through so many of these interviews that she'd lost count. It was as if her father were punishing her by conducting them all in a single day. Each one as boring as the last and she wasn't sure how her father expected her to choose any of them. The first thing her father had mentioned was his disappointment in her choice of clothes, he'd hoped she would try a little harder, he'd said. She felt an aching in her chest as she sat in her seat beside him, an emptiness beginning to consume her. She had thought she could make her father see reason, but now she wasn't so sure.

One after another, the princes entered, putting on their most charming smiles, their fanciest clothes, bringing in extravagant gifts that she was supposed to swoon over, but they were all essentially the same; shiny trinkets designed to buy her affection. Not one of these princes caught her attention, not one said a single interesting thing or seemed to care that her father was doing most of the talking and she had yet to open her mouth.

All the men in the room seemed to prefer that, even as she felt like she was slowly dying inside. The only one who seemed concerned was Jafar, who she was refusing to look at, so she scowled every time she caught his eye.

She tried to think of something else. Aladdin's face came to mind again, his easy smile, the mischief in his eyes, the way he'd saved her from that merchant and run with her from the guards. He hadn't treated her like a useless woman, he hadn't treated her like an object to be bartered for. She wanted to see him again. Her heart raced at the very thought.

This time when she caught Jafar's eyes, he was the one scowling, though she had no idea why. Had he guessed her thoughts? Had he already caught on to her plans of escape? Surely not. It was only her guilty conscience, he didn't know her well enough to know her thoughts, and no one would suspect she was bold enough to escape again so soon.

Tonight, she would find Aladdin again, and she would ask him to show her the city she wasn't allowed to see.

The last prince bowed low and left the room, seeming pleased with himself, as if he thought the meeting went well. But as the door closed, her father sighed. 'That will be enough today, I believe the princess is tired.'

The sun was low in the sky and Jasmine was glad to finally be free. She bowed to her father, ensuring she appeared defeated. She couldn't have anyone catching on too soon, before she'd had a chance to really see the city. As soon as she was out of sight, she hurried as fast as her feet would carry her. She needed to change, but this time, she would borrow some of Lina's clothes to ensure she was harder to detect.

Excitement bubbled in her stomach at that gloriously familiar sensation of doing something she shouldn't. Soon they would learn that she would never be controlled.

Jasmine snuck out of the palace under the cover of darkness, her stomach giddy with excitement. She'd convinced Lina to lend her some clothes, and though they were still fine, no one would mistake her for a princess.

The marketplace was easy enough to find, with a raging fire in the centre of the square and music filling the night. Her eyes widened as she took in the sight of the people dancing, the merriment and drinking. She wondered if they were celebrating something as she walked around, looking at everything as though she'd never seen it before.

'Jasmine?' a familiar voice said, sounding shocked. She turned to find Aladdin bounding towards her, a bright smile on his face, and it was perhaps the first time since her mother's passing that someone had been genuinely happy to see her.

'Are you surprised?' she asked, unable to stop from smiling back.

'I heard the guards took you. I didn't think you'd be able to sneak out again so soon,' he said. 'But I'm glad you did.'

Her cheeks warmed. Was she blushing?

'Come on,' he said, as if he hadn't even noticed. He took her hand as if it was the most natural thing in the world, and led her into the fray of dancing bodies. She'd never danced with such a large group of people before, but the music soon coaxed her hips to move, her body swaying and spinning, the steps coming easily to her until finally she just let go. The merriment of her people was catching and she found herself smiling wide as she danced with Aladdin.

Her mind suddenly wandered back to that night she'd danced with Jafar, that intense heat she'd felt, the one that threatened to take her breath away. When she danced with Aladdin, she didn't feel that same intensity, she felt something else, an easy freedom. She found herself wanting to dance all night, but she also felt like something was missing. She shook the thought from her mind and focused on the dance. She didn't know when she would have the chance to do this again.

Chapter 7

Jafar

The look in Princess Jasmine's eyes had troubled Jafar. There was something wistful about it, something like longing that stirred an ugly feeling in his chest, instantly souring his mood. Why did it bother him so much? She'd tried to hide it but she was too eager to leave, too quiet, too compliant. She was up to something.

And the way she'd refused to look at him was torture.

He paced in his chambers. Patience was not one of his strong suits, he was well aware. Now, however, he had no choice but to wait for the princess to make her move. She may want to rule the kingdom, but she showed her inexperience at every turn.

'My lord,' a man said in hushed tones. Jafar turned to face the man who bowed before him, keeping his head low. 'She has left the palace and heads towards the market.'

'Thank you,' Jafar said, dismissing the man. Now the game was afoot.

He snuck from the palace on a well-travelled route lit by crude torches, down dark stairwells and passageways long since forgotten. He exited into the night, heading for the marketplace, which even at that late hour thrived;

moonlight drowned out by a huge fire, wine flowing freely, dancing and merriment all around. It had been the same when he was a boy, sometimes he would go to watch, sometimes the other boys would steal the wine and join the festivities, if they didn't get flogged and chased off first.

But he knew she would love this.

He spotted her then, dressed in her maid's clothes, as if that could hide her, make her less noticeable. Wherever she went, she would be noticed, her beauty could not be hidden so easily. She was looking for something or someone. The idea of her meeting some man here on a secret tryst made his blood boil and he stepped forward to make his presence known.

But he stopped dead as a man bounded towards her. He looked around her age, youthful, the kind of man who wasn't weighed down with the burden of responsibility. Despite being young, he was scruffy, clearly an urchin, a street rat. What could the princess possibly see in the likes of him?

That ugly feeling roiled inside him as she smiled at the street rat, a dazzling smile that she had never shown to him. Jafar moved closer, keeping to the shadows as they walked around the market, her face showing her delight at everything. The street rat took her hand as if it was the most natural thing in the world and she didn't shy away from him. He led her to the dancers and they joined in the merriment, the princess laughing joyously.

Jafar's hands balled into fists so tight his knuckles turned white and the scales of his staff bit into his flesh. Had the urchin so easily won her heart? He had nothing to offer her and yet she had left the palace for him, knowing the consequences should she be caught. Something had to be done and he knew exactly what that something was. A smirk tugged at his lips as he watched the pair dance, knowing that it would only be for tonight.

Princess Jasmine had finally returned to the castle, staying much later than he would have liked. That poor street rat was half in love with her already, and Jafar didn't like it one bit. While Iago stayed to watch the boy, Jafar had travelled to the enchanted cave to wait. It had been a long time since he'd done his own dirty work, but this was something he needed to see to himself.

Soon he heard the hoofbeats of a horse and he rose from the ground, brushing sand from his robes. Iago dropped the street rat unceremoniously at his feet before jumping off the horse himself.

Jafar raised an eyebrow at the man, noting a gash on his cheek. The street rat had clearly put up a fight, so he didn't begrudge Iago his anger. 'Did you knock him out or kill him?' Jafar asked. Honestly, he would have been satisfied with either scenario, the result was the same.

'I could kill him, if you like, master,' Iago sneered, eyeing the street rat hungrily.

A tempting offer but Jafar wanted to savour the boy's destruction. 'What is his name?' he asked as he peered down at the unconscious boy, not understanding at all what Jasmine had seen in him.

'Aladdin.'

Jafar sighed and took a seat once more in the sand as he waited for Aladdin to come to, though he hoped it wouldn't take too long. He needed to get back to the palace. 'I don't suppose you can wake him?'

Iago looked positively ropable. If anything might actually tempt the man to turn on him, it might be this. Jafar let it go and lay back, his eyes cast at the stars in the heavens above as they sparkled brightly against a sea of black. His mind once again turned to Princess Jasmine. What did she see in this boy? If she had to stoop below her station, could she not have stopped at him?

What a thought. As if the sultan would allow it.

As if *he* had time for it.

And yet, he couldn't shake these feelings she had stirred to life in him. She needed to marry a prince, it was the easiest way to secure Agrabah's future, though it wasn't the *only* way. If, in some alternate reality, she chose him, he could make it work, he could make Agrabah safe for her. With the lamp in his possession, it would be a simple task.

But she wouldn't choose him. Couldn't. There was not a single example from history wherein a princess of Agrabah had married so below her station.

And yet he couldn't seem to turn his mind from it.

The street rat began to stir, groaning as his consciousness returned. Jafar sat up, staring at the young man whose eyes suddenly snapped open. He started, stumbling back across the sand.

'Who are you? What do you want?' he asked, fear evident in his voice. Jafar supposed a thief would make plenty of enemies if he lived long enough.

'I apologise for the manner in which you were brought here,' Jafar said, plastering on his most diplomatic expression, even as he wanted to throw the boy into the cave and never think about him again. 'I think that we are in a position to help each other.'

Aladdin sat up then, scrutinising Jafar as if the boy could ever know what was going on in his mind. 'Who are you?' he asked. There was a caution in his voice but also a curiosity. This was going to be too easy.

'My name is Jafar.'

Aladdin's eyes widened. 'The sultan's advisor?'

Jafar smiled then. 'The very same. And it has come to my attention that you have certain...interests in our princess.' It took a considerable amount of effort to keep his emotions in check as he spoke those words, his instincts screaming at him to cease this ploy and throttle the whelp already.

'What? Princess? I don't –' Aladdin stammered, eyes darting nervously.

Jafar tilted his head, raising an eyebrow. 'For a thief, I expected you to be a better liar.' Aladdin said nothing, but he wouldn't meet Jafar's gaze either. Was he a coward or was he smart? It was hard to tell. 'As I said before, I believe there's a way for us to help each other.'

'How?' Aladdin asked, scepticism in his voice.

'There is something I need, and it's in that cave over there,' Jafar said, nodding towards the entrance. 'It requires someone of your...skillset. Get it for me, and I will make you rich enough to impress a princess.'

Aladdin mulled over his words carefully, but Jafar recognised the greed in his eyes. There was only one answer the street rat could give. 'What am I stealing?'

Jafar smiled. 'Inside the cave are many treasures, you must not touch anything except for a golden lamp.'

'What makes this lamp so special?' Aladdin asked.

'That's my business. All you need to do is get it for me and I'll make you rich. That is our deal.'

Aladdin nodded, clearly thinking he had the better end of the deal. Simple minded fool. Jafar led him to the gaping mouth of the cave. It didn't go back very far, but at the entrance was a steep slope with misshapen stones which would almost be seen as a makeshift stairway. Whether it was manmade or something natural, he didn't know. No one really know how old the cave was. He watched as the street rat descended, he watched until the darkness swallowed him.

Now all he had to do was wait. Either the street rat would return with the lamp as promised, or he would die down there as all the others had. Jafar was leaning towards the latter, perhaps out of jealousy, perhaps out of logic, who could say, really?

Iago stood by the horses, a sour look still on his face as the moon climbed higher into the night. Jafar kept his eyes on the mouth of the cave, unsure of which outcome he was more excited for. Suddenly, the Earth began to rumble and he knew that Aladdin had not heeded his warning. He'd touched something he shouldn't have. Idiot boy. Well, there would be no lamp tonight, but at least the street rat wouldn't be a problem anymore. He was about to leave when he saw the street rat climbing up to the entrance. He gripped the edge, his teeth gritted with the effort.

'Give me your hand!' he cried in desperation.

'First, give me the lamp,' Jafar said coldly. Aladdin looked up in horror as he realised his situation, that Jafar would let him die without batting an eye, and it set a sense of satisfaction aglow in Jafar's chest.

The street rat held out the lamp and Jafar snatched it from him, eyeing it with glee. He finally had it in his hands, he finally possessed the magic lamp.

'Your hand!' Aladdin yelled.

Jafar looked down at him, unmoved by the young man's plea. The man who sought to take Princess Jasmine, the man who sorely did not deserve her. 'No, I don't think so.'

'But I got you the lamp!'

'Yes, you did,' Jafar said. He turned to leave but he felt a hand clamp around his ankle. Aladdin nimbly manoeuvred himself in a way Jafar hadn't expected, and he snatched the lamp from Jafar's belt before he went hurtling back into the abyss.

'Damn it!' Jafar roared, anger raging inside him. He'd been so close, he almost had the lamp in his possession but he'd let his emotions cloud his judgement. That blasted woman had ruined it all for him! His obsession with her was becoming unbearable, consuming him like a raging fire, destroying logic and reason. And now the lamp was once again out of his reach.

Chapter 8

Jasmine

J asmine sat on the edge of the fountain, the cool stone a stark contrast to the warm evening air. The moon was high in the sky, shining brilliantly across the water's surface. When she was a girl, she used to take off her shoes, hike up her skirts and jump into that fountain, splashing water everywhere. Her mother had caught her once, a look of shock on her face which had quickly been replaced by mischief and she, the queen of Agrabah, had taken off her shoes and hiked up her skirts to join her wild daughter.

She smiled to herself at the memory. She wondered what her father would have done if he'd known his wife was just as wild. Would he be more understanding towards her now?

She let out a sigh.

She was expected to choose a husband from those on offer, as if she were choosing a new pair of shoes. And if she didn't choose, would her father choose for her? Who would he pick if she did not?

She shook the thought from her mind. Tonight Aladdin was coming. She'd doubted him when he'd said he would visit her, but he seemed sure he could, though he wouldn't say how he planned to slip past the guards.

She'd dressed well for the occasion, even though she knew he wouldn't know the difference. She'd done it because she was nervous, though of what she couldn't quite say. Jafar's face came to mind again. She couldn't help comparing him to Aladdin. Aladdin had a youthful face, a boyish charm that made her worries melt away. Jafar was all intensity and darkness, he had the handsomeness of a man, the hardness of one who had seen much, and there was something about him that set her stomach fluttering. She wondered what would happen if he caught her there in that garden with a man. Would he care beyond his duty? Did she want him to?

'Are you waiting for someone, princess?' his dark voice rumbled, as if she'd summoned him with her thoughts.

She looked up to find him standing in the archway, his black robes immaculate, only tonight he didn't hold his sceptre in hand. It was the first time she'd seen him without it. His eyes seemed darker than usual, that intensity in their gaze ever present, sending a shiver through her.

'What makes you think so?' she asked vaguely, tearing her eyes away from him to stare into the water as it glistened in the moonlight, lilies swaying gently on the surface.

'You've dressed a little too nicely for a stroll through the gardens alone,' he said, somewhat bitterly. 'Did one of the princes finally catch your eye?'

'You'd like that, wouldn't you,' she said coldly, looking back at him, surprised to find him walking towards her. He was closing the distance between them with every step.

He stopped before her, tilting his head, a silent struggle in his eyes that made her forget her anger for a moment. 'And if I told you I wouldn't?'

Her heart sped up in her chest, she couldn't tear her eyes away. A voice in the back of her mind told her to move, to send him away, she was expecting someone else this night, but she couldn't find the words. 'What are you saying?' she asked, her voice sounding breathy to her ears, like it wasn't her voice at all.

What was *she* saying? Was she encouraging this? She stood quickly, in an attempt to put some distance between them so she could think but her feet wouldn't move, her eyes trapped in his. He reached out a hand and for the first time in her life, she saw hesitation in this confident man who always knew his path as clear as if it had been marked out on a map for him. His fingers touched her jaw, a featherlight touch that sent a spark of warmth into her skin.

His fingers slid up her jaw, as if he was getting use to the feel of her skin, as if he was learning her face and her eyes fluttered closed as she leaned into his touch. He froze and her eyes snapped open, a blush rising to her cheeks. What was she doing?

'Um, I should...' she mumbled and she tried to step around him, but his hand caught her wrist in a firm grip. When she looked up at him, his eyes were dark with desire and something more she couldn't put her finger on.

'Who did you dress for tonight?' he asked, a dark edge to his voice.

'Are you jealous, Jafar?' she asked, relieved that her confidence had returned.

His hand tightened around her wrist. 'Why? Are you trying to make me jealous, princess?' he countered. He pulled her to him, the smallest movement sending her tumbling to his chest. His breath smelled sweet like wine. Had he been drinking? Is that why he was acting this way? Or was it something more?

'I feel as if you have enchanted me,' he said softly, his hand cupping her face. Then his lips brushed against hers, lightly at first, testing. Her breath hitched in her throat and a warmth exploded in her core. Her hands gripped his robes as he deepened the kiss, his hand on her waist pulling her tightly against him, his lips claiming hers with such passion, his hand cupping the back of her neck. Her body tingled with pleasure and a moan escaped her throat.

Suddenly coming to her senses, she pushed away from him, her chest heaving with every breath. What was she *doing*? She was supposed to be waiting for Aladdin, and here she was with Jafar. Why didn't she want to stop?

Anger flashed like a storm in his dark eyes as she was trying to gather her thoughts. 'Do you think *he* is enough to satisfy you?' he demanded.

Did he know about Aladdin? No, he couldn't possibly. Could he?

What business was it of his, anyway?

'And you think you are?' she countered, her own anger rising to meet his.

He took a strong step towards her and she took one back, he met her step for step until her back pressed against the stone wall and she had nowhere left to go, that darkness growing deeper in his eyes. He slammed one palm against the wall beside her head, caging her in, then leaned close, only inches away from her, his breath caressing her skin, her heart racing wildly in her chest., A warm throbbing began between her legs and all she could think about was his lips on hers.

'Princess, I'm the *only* one who can,' he said in a rumbling voice full of confidence that made her breath hitch in her throat.

She raised her chin, standing tall to face him. 'Prove it,' she said, her previous anger replaced with an undeniable desire.

He gripped her chin between his thumb and forefinger. 'You should be careful what you say to men,' he warned, his voice a low growl.

'Or what?' she countered as she stared into the intensity of those dark eyes, drawing her in, threatening to drown her, and she didn't care. She didn't care if he consumed her body and soul, in that moment all she wanted was to feel him.

His lips crashed to hers, fierce and dominating, her chin still gripped in his fingers, his arm on the wall was the only thing keeping any distance between them. She found herself resenting that arm, wanting him to press himself against her, wanting to feel what he had beneath those robes.

The sound of footsteps and jangling metal brought her back to reality, and Jafar sprang away from her, a look of confusion on his face which was quickly replaced by a scowl. She tried to get her breathing under control as she watched his transformation, her brain struggling to comprehend. The guards responsible for the noise marched passed, oblivious to the moment they had just trampled on.

'You should not linger here, princess,' Jafar said, then he turned on his heels and disappeared as quickly as he had appeared, leaving her feeling more confused than ever.

Angrier than ever.

She could feel the familiar prick of tears in her eyes and she clenched her teeth. She would not cry for *him*. She straightened her shoulders and brushed out her dress before walking back to her chambers as if nothing had happened.

She closed the door with a heavy thud, her mind still in turmoil as she stared into the distance.

'Did he show?' Lina asked excitedly.

'What? Who?' Jasmine asked distractedly, guilt finding its way into her words as if she'd be caught doing something she really ought not to be doing. And Jafar was definitely one of those things she ought not to be doing.

Lina frowned at her in confusion. 'The boy from the market? The one who said he was going to break into the palace to see you.'

'Oh, uh...no, he didn't show,' Jasmine said as she watched the frown deepen on her handmaid's face.

'Alright, spill. What happened?' Lina asked crossing her arms.

'Excuse me, I am your princess,' Jasmine said, trying her best to deflect but her heart was still racing, her skin still burning from his touch.

Lina simply raised an eyebrow. 'This is exactly why you chose me, don't get all prudish and pull rank on me.'

Jasmine sunk her teeth into her lip as she thought. She wasn't ready to out herself but she felt like she might explode if she didn't say *something*. What had just happened? Why had he run off? Did he regret it? Did she?

She should. He had a reputation that had taken her all of a day to uncover as ruthless and cold, though his advice to the sultan was infallible, a source of great bitterness to the men beneath him, especially those who were much older.

He was not at all like the boy she'd known before, and she found that thrilling. Too thrilling.

'I'm not letting this go, so you had better tell me or there won't be anything for you to eat tomorrow, I'll have died of curiosity,' Lina said dramatically.

Jasmine looked at her in exasperation. 'People don't die of curiosity.'

'Oh yes they do, what about all those explorers who go missing or –'

'Stop, please just stop,' Jasmine begged.

Lina pumped her fist in victory, then sat on the bed and looked up at her eagerly. It was hard not to think of the girl as the sister she never had. And she was right, it was why Jasmine had chosen her.

Jasmine sat on the bed, unable to look at Lina any longer. Guilt and shame twisted in her. Not because she'd kissed Jafar, not because she'd wanted him, but because she didn't feel ashamed of it, though she knew she should. 'Aladdin didn't show up tonight. Jafar did,' she said slowly, waiting for her handmaid to berate her as anyone else would in the palace.

'Jafar? As in tall, dark, and sexy?' Lina said, her jaw dropping.

Sometimes Jasmine forgot that Lina didn't grow up in the palace as she had. But she wasn't surprised that her handmaid knew of Jafar's reputation as well as anyone else.

Lina had a gift for uncovering all the necessary gossip in a matter of minutes.

'Don't look at me like that, I like them that way,' Lina said and let out a dreamy sigh.

'Has anyone ever told you you're strange?'

'Yep. So, what happened?'

The kiss replayed in Jasmine's mind, that all-consuming moment of passion before he'd jumped away from her as if he'd been burned and fled. 'I don't...know,' she said as she replayed the scene again and again, her heart aching a little more each time.

'You do know, now spill or I will have to fill in the blanks with the naughtiest details I can think of.'

'It was just a kiss, it doesn't mean anything,' Jasmine snapped quickly, shutting down the imaginings that came with Lina's words. She could feel her cheeks beginning to grow warm.

Lina gasped dramatically. 'He kissed you?'

Jasmine nodded. It was more than a kiss, it was all intensity and passion, forbidden and addictive. She'd lost herself in that kiss, in him, wanting things she shouldn't want. Was it really just a kiss or was there something else, some spark of connection that had ignited between them?

But he wasn't exactly in line for her hand. Her father had arranged for a number of men to please her enough to accept them, and Jafar would never be among those numbers.

Out the corner of her eye she could see Lina's face drop, a sadness sweeping over her expression. Jasmine fell back against the mattress and stared up at the ceiling. 'Would it be so bad?' Lina asked.

'What?'

'Marrying Jafar.'

Jasmine looked at her then, brows furrowed. Marry Jafar? Was there something written on her face? 'He's not a prince,' Jasmine said, sidestepping the question. Because the worst thing was that it *wouldn't* be so bad, would it? She'd felt more connected to him than any other. No one else made her heart race the way he did, no one else made that warmth blossom in her core, no one else looked at her the way he did.

And that only made her heart ache when she remembered that she would be forced to marry someone else. Perhaps it would be better to try and push him from her mind completely, to try and focus on the options available to her or to refuse to marry at all, though she suspected that her father would force the issue at some point.

'But the sultan would be amenable, I think. He wants you to be safe, he wants the kingdom to be in good hands. Jafar has been running the kingdom at his side for years,' Lina reasoned.

And she made a terrifying amount of sense. Her father did trust and respect him, and he certainly had the experience to rule Agrabah. But would Jafar let her rule at his side? Doubtful. He was helping her father palm her off onto some man because women aren't meant to rule.

Why were they even talking about this? He obviously wasn't thinking about it. He'd not put his name forward, he'd not spoken to her or the sultan. In fact, he seemed to be resisting the entire situation. Had he regretted kissing her? He'd certainly run off fast enough.

'You are way too excited. I'm taking a bath,' Jasmine said, jumping up from the bed and marching to the bathroom, slamming the door before Lina could follow. She needed to clear her head, to think of anything else.

As she stared at the empty bath, wondering if she could fill it herself, her mind again replayed the kiss in the gardens under the beautiful moonlight and the intensity in his eyes. She pressed her fingers to her lips as if she could still feel him there, then let out a heavy sigh.

What the hell was she doing?

Chapter 9

Aladdin

A laddin's eyes snapped open in the almost pitch-black darkness of the cave, pain radiating along his back, but otherwise he seemed unharmed. He should have known that bastard would double-cross him. How many times had his father warned him *if a situation is too good to be true, Aladdin, then it probably is*? Hadn't he learnt first-hand the underhandedness of the rich and powerful?

He clenched his fists in anger and metal bit into his flesh. He looked down to see he still held the lamp in his hand. A deranged chuckle left his throat. Jafar might have double-crossed him, but he hadn't won the game. Would he come back for the lamp? Would that be his way out? But then, what would stop Jafar from trying to kill him again? Perhaps the next time, he would succeed.

What made this thing so special?

His eyes slowly began to adjust to the darkness. There was light coming from somewhere, so there must be a way out. He had to find it or he'd die down here in this rotten cave. Honestly, how was he supposed to know that touching the treasure would lead to this? Was it so wrong to want a little something extra for his troubles? The necklace had been beautiful, and he knew Jasmine would have loved it. It would be the perfect gift to win her heart. Women loved crap like that. Whenever his mother was mad, all his father had to do was present her with a trinket and all was forgiven. That necklace was more than a mere trinket, it was fit for a princess.

Aladdin let out a sigh. This was exactly why he never coveted anything he couldn't readily grab. The first rule of being a thief, never attempt to steal something that isn't a sure thing – it will likely get you killed. It was one of the reasons he'd survived so long. He never took more than he needed, never took anything to draw attention to himself.

The one time he'd broken that rule and he was going to pay for it with his life.

Jafar could have been a little less cryptic in his warning. Hell, the bastard could have *helped him out of the fucking cave*. Why would he throw Aladdin back in? Well, the joke was on him, because Aladdin had the lamp he wanted so badly, the one he was apparently ready to kill for.

Even if he was trapped down there with it.

A single shaft of light penetrated the darkness and Aladdin held the lamp up to it. It was a pretty thing, he supposed, probably worth a good amount of gold. It was, after all, made of gold with intricate carvings, though the metal was tarnished. If he cleaned it up a bit, would he see what made it worth so much to Jafar? He rubbed his sleeve over the dull metal, attempting to polish it, when the lamp began to heat in his hands. A blue smoke began to pour out of the spout and he dropped it in surprise as the smoke kept coming, creating a huge blue cloud before him.

'Who has summoned the Djinn of the lamp?' a deep voice rumbled from within the blue smoke.

Aladdin's eyes went wide, a shiver of fear crawling up his spine. 'A Djinn?' he asked, dumbfounded. No wonder Jafar had wanted this thing so badly, just think of all the things he could do with a Djinn at his beck and call!

A face appeared as the smoke dissipated, then a torso, though the rest of the Djinn's body seemed to be made of mist. He was huge, big enough to send men cowering, with wide shoulders and bulging muscles. His jaw was strong and square, dark stubble coating it, a stark contrast against his blue skin.

The Djinn raised his eyebrow at Aladdin, his gaze sweeping over him as if sizing him up, then he smirked, having clearly made his assessment. 'So, young master,' he said, then looked about them. 'Care to make your first wish?'

'How many wishes do I get?' Aladdin asked.

The Djinn looked at him as if he was an idiot. 'Three,' he said in his deep voice. It seemed he wasn't about to offer any more words than were absolutely necessary.

The Djinn obviously expected Aladdin to waste a wish getting out of that cave. But Aladdin never paid for anything he could get for free. He certainly wasn't going to waste something as valuable as a wish.

Aladdin thought for a moment, then looked sceptically at the Djinn. 'Wishes, huh? Are you sure you're a Djinn?'

A displeased expression settled on the Djinn's face as he glared down at Aladdin. 'What else would I be?'

Aladdin shrugged. 'I don't know. I've never met a Djinn before. Prove it. Prove to me that you are what you say,' he said, doing his best to act nonchalant. People underestimated him all the time because of his age. It was something he used to his advantage at every turn.

'If you don't want your wishes, simply leave the cave. Or have you lost your way?' the Djinn asked with a smirk, his rumbling voice mocking.

But Aladdin wasn't ready to give up yet. 'How long has it been, Djinn, since you've been stuck in this cave?'

'Do you think mortals haven't tried this ruse before, boy?' the Djinn asked, inspecting his nails.

Aladdin supposed it wasn't exactly an original move. An immortal Djinn had probably seen much. Aladdin decided to change tactics. 'I was betrayed and trapped in his place, surely you can get us out of here. Then I can make my first wish.'

'And why would I do that?' the Djinn asked, raising an eyebrow. But Aladdin knew he had the Djinn's attention now.

'If you get us out of here without a wish, then I will grant you free reign outside – you can come and go from the lamp as you please. Though you would need to...blend in,' Aladdin said, taking in the Djinn's half human form.

The Djinn smiled to himself. 'You are a particularly insolent mortal. Very well. I will get us out of this cave, and you will make your first wish.'

Aladdin was surprised the Djinn agreed but he wasn't about to look a gift horse in the mouth. He kept his expression schooled against the surge of triumph he felt, lest the Djinn change his mind.

The Djinn snapped his fingers and Aladdin's vision was engulfed in blue smoke. When it cleared, he was on the sand outside the cave, the sun burning down on him. How long had he been in that cave? How long had he lain there unconscious? He was supposed to meet with Jasmine, he'd told her to wait for him, boasted that he could break into the palace with ease. Had he missed their rendezvous? Would she be disappointed he hadn't shown?

'Your wish,' the Djinn said with complete disinterest, interrupting Aladdin's thoughts.

'I can wish for anything?' Aladdin asked.

The Djinn sighed in exasperation. 'You can't wish for more wishes, I can't kill anyone or bring anyone back from the dead, and I can't make anyone fall in love with you,' he said, ticking each one off on his long blue fingers.

He could wish for almost anything, those rules really didn't affect him at all. He had no one he desperately needed to bring back from the dead, the only person he might want to kill is Jafar, but there were far better ways to get revenge on the advisor. He'd simply need to do his homework first.

But when he thought about what he wanted most in the world, Princess Jasmine's face came to mind.

'So, I can wish for you to make me a prince?' Aladdin asked.

The Djinn raised his eyebrow again before hiking his shoulders. 'Sure, kid, but why would you want to be a prince?'

'There's a princess, but she can only marry a prince. Her father has been bringing in suitors for the past week,' Aladdin said, smiling as he remembered Jasmine's face at the marketplace, dancing around the fire with the light shining off her silky hair, her eyes filled with laughter.

'I told you I can't make anyone fall in love with you.'

'I know, I don't need you to. We had a connection. I just, need to be a prince,' Aladdin said.

The Djinn looked at him, waiting. Finally, he waved a big blue hand in prompt.

'Oh, right. Djinn, I wish to become a prince,' Aladdin said, excitement squeezing his chest.

Blue smoke engulfed his vision once more and a warm feeling spread through his body as a grin spread across his face. Jafar had failed to kill him and had actually given him the means to have the most beautiful woman in the land. He had given him the means to become the richest man in the kingdom; from pauper to sultan, a transformation no one would have suspected.

When the smoke cleared, he was dressed in the finest clothes he'd ever seen, brilliant white and trimmed with gold. A thought occurred to him then. If Jafar was the sultan's advisor, then he was bound to run into him sooner or later. He was betting sooner.

'Won't people recognise me?' he asked.

The Djinn shook his head. 'No one will recognise you, that's how the magic works.'

Jafar wouldn't know it was him, but neither would Jasmine. He'd have to woo her all over again, but he'd done it once, he knew they had a connection. He could do it again. He grinned to himself.

'Let's get to the palace.'

Chapter 10

Jafar

The sultan was pacing when Jafar entered the small room, the large feather in his hat bobbing with each step. Well, it was small by comparison to most of the other rooms in the palace. The sultan called this particular room his planning room, something about it made him feel calm, and who was Jafar to argue with the sultan? Besides, he was also fond of it, private, away from prying eyes and scornful looks.

'Ah, Jafar! There you are,' the sultan said, a hurried greeting accompanied by a furrowed brow. At least the pacing had ceased.

'You seem troubled, your majesty,' Jafar said, stating the obvious. It wasn't hard to guess what was troubling the man, it seemed the princess was determined not to choose a husband.

His mind flashed back to the night before last, Princess Jasmine waiting in the courtyard dressed to perfection. Waiting for a man, a thief no doubt. The sight of her sitting there, knowing she was waiting for that street rat made his blood boil. Before he could stop himself he was in that garden, and when her eyes had met his, he hadn't been able to resist. Wine had made him more susceptible to his baser desires. He'd needed to taste her, just once.

Fatal last words.

Now that he had tasted her lips, he knew that once was never going to be enough. He could barely keep her from his mind. She haunted his every waking moment, she possessed his every dream, and all the while he had to sit in that room and watch as she was introduced to one man after another in the hopes that one would pique her interest and take her away from him forever.

'You seem distracted, Jafar,' the sultan said, interrupting his thoughts.

'You as well, your majesty,' Jafar said, deflecting skilfully, though he'd scarcely had occasion to do so in the past. This woman was consuming him in a way no one ever had before, eroding his logic, his sanity.

'It's Jasmine. She's just being so difficult. Every prince I've put before her she's rejected, and we are running out of kingdoms,' the sultan huffed in exasperation, returning to his pacing.

'You could always choose for her,' Jafar forced himself to bite out, the words feeling like acid clawing at his throat.

The sultan let out a heavy sigh, placing his plump hands on the table, staring into the map stretched out there as if it held all the answers. 'I...I can't do that to her. Her mother would never forgive me.'

Relief washed through him and he resisted the urge to scowl at himself for his foolishness. Did he suppose that left her for him? She *had* kissed him back, but did that mean he had her heart? He shouldn't want her heart. She was meant for someone else, someone with the loyalty of a kingdom attached to his hand.

'Then we will just have to think of another plan,' Jafar said. 'Perhaps there is another way to secure the kingdom without marriage to one of our neighbours.'

It would involve strengthening relationships with their allies; perhaps a trade agreement, some expensive gifts, some extravagant parties, a little leverage here or there. Not as easy as a marriage but significantly more interesting. And with Princess Jasmine free and unattached –

The sound of drums in the distance interrupted his thoughts, capturing the sultan's attention. The pair of them moved to the balcony as the sound grew louder. When they looked out over the city, they could see a shock of colour moving towards them. Dancers, musicians, and elephants, one in particular covered in the finest décor and no doubt carrying the man responsible for the gaudy display, though the sultan seemed to be enjoying himself, bobbing along to the music with a smile on his face.

They weren't expecting any more princes, so who was this man?

As the parade neared, he could see a man throwing coins into the cheering crowd that had gathered along the sides of the street to see the display. He had a wide smile on his face and there was something strangely familiar about him, though Jafar couldn't quite place him, which immediately incited his suspicion.

The man in question looked up at the palace and Jafar followed his gaze. Princess Jasmine was watching from her balcony, too, though she didn't seem to share her father's enthusiasm. She ached an elegant eyebrow at the display, her displeasure invoking a satisfaction in Jafar's chest. When the man waved at her, flashing a charming smile, she rolled her eyes and disappeared back inside. A smug smile curled Jafar's lips.

'Quickly, let's go and receive him,' the sultan said eagerly. 'I have a good feeling about this one.'

Jafar couldn't share in the sultan's optimism, after seeing the princess's reaction to the newcomer, and also because he had begun to secretly covet her for himself, something he would have to curb quickly if he hoped to keep his sanity and the position he'd worked so hard for.

He followed the sultan into the throne room, taking his place to the right. They waited, the sultan showing signs of impatience as Jafar concentrated on keeping perfectly still to hide his own. The doors opened wide and the announcer called, 'Prince Ali of Lingden.'

Lingden? The last Jafar had heard, Lingden had only three princesses. Would they have hidden a son and heir from the world? Perhaps he was disgraced, and not the heir at all. Though that seemed contradictory to the king's personality. The man was boastful to a fault, he would not have...Jafar's mind grew hazy, as if something had snatched the thought from him, and he couldn't seem to grasp it back.

'Prince Ali,' the sultan said, smiling wide. 'That was quite the entrance.'

Prince Ali smiled back, though his was the cocky smile of youth. That sense of familiarity gnawed at Jafar, though he still couldn't place the boy. Jafar prided himself on his memory, he never forgot a face, so why did this prince elude him?

The prince wore fine white clothes trimmed in gold, his dark hair was short and tousled, his skin dark and smooth, as would be expected if he had lived in a palace his entire life. He was certainly attractive, Jafar had to admit, but then, some of the others had been just as attractive and still the princess had turned them away.

Would she turn Prince Ali away too? He couldn't put his finger on what bothered him so much about this prince. Did he stand a chance of winning the princess's heart and taking her from him?

What was he thinking? She wasn't *his*, the prince had just as much claim on her as he did. That thought sat sourly with him, that ugly feeling returning to nestle in his chest again.

'I'm sure the princess will be down momentarily,' the sultan said, bringing Jafar back to the present. 'We had thought the King of Lingden would not send a son.'

Prince Ali laughed somewhat awkwardly. 'You must forgive my late arrival. I had not thought I stood a chance.'

'Yes, many have sought my daughter's hand, though none have been able to win it,' the sultan said almost proudly, despite the fact that the entire purpose of these last days had been to accomplish exactly that.

'Word of her beauty has spread across the land, you must be very proud,' Prince Ali simpered.

Princess Jasmine chose that moment to enter the room. She had clearly put thought into her clothes, choosing a royal blue, fierce and brilliant, clad around her. She stood tall, her displeasure evident on her face. She didn't look like a princess in that moment, she looked like a queen, and for the first time, Jafar really could see her sitting on her father's throne, ruling the kingdom – with the right guiding hands, of course.

Perhaps that was his own selfish desire speaking.

'It seems that Prince Ali has only come to claim a beautiful trinket,' the princess sneered coldly. 'Are you looking for a bauble to decorate your throne?'

'I – uh...that's not what I meant, princess,' Prince Ali stammered, looking somewhat confused.

'I am only a woman, after all, what more could I desire than to be deemed beautiful by a man?' she said drolly.

'Jasmine, that's enough,' the sultan snapped, and she clamped her mouth shut with an audible click, a frown sitting firmly on her face. 'I apologise, Prince Ali, this has been very...trying on the princess.'

Prince Ali smiled awkwardly. 'Yes, it must be a difficult position. I, too, have expectations on my marriage, though I have more options open to me. It hardly seems fair.'

Princess Jasmine raised an eyebrow, a small movement that lasted only a moment but Jafar hadn't missed it. The prince had said something that impressed her, clearly a calculated move. Jafar ground his teeth. Would she fall for such trickery?

He needed to relinquish any perceived claim he had on her. He had none, he was only an advisor. Once, that position had been enough for him, but over the last few days it had begun to feel lacking as his eyes found her in every room they were in, looking for her everywhere she was not.

He would be glad when the princess rejected this new suitor and there was no one left to tempt her. If he couldn't have her, at least he needn't watch her with someone else.

Chapter 11

Jasmine

Jasmine returned to her room in a foul mood when she was finally released from the throne room, and she stormed back to her chambers. Prince Ali had marched into Agrabah with his ridiculous parade, and her father had been all too accommodating, welcoming him inside despite the fact he hadn't been invited. And the way he'd spoken to the sultan, he'd managed to do what none of the others had. In just a few hours he'd charmed her father so completely that she worried her resistance wouldn't matter anymore.

Lina's eyebrows shot up when Jasmine entered, shutting the door forcefully behind her. 'The meeting didn't go well, then?' her handmaid asked as if she already knew the answer.

'Why are we still *having* these meetings? I thought I had sat through the posturing of every pompous arse in the land. Where did this Prince Ali come from?' Jasmine snapped.

'Did you think your father would have let you rule alone if you rejected them all?' Lina asked, tilting her head as if Jasmine were being idiotic. Maybe she was.

Jasmine let out a heavy sigh. 'I don't know.'

'Surely you could do worse than this one?' Lina offered. 'Your father seems very fond of him.'

'How do you know that?' Jasmine asked, surprised. Her father had liked him, a lot. He was smiling a lot and that hopeful look had entered his eyes. She worried that if she rejected Prince Ali, her father would simply force the issue and there would be nothing she could do about it.

Lina scoffed. 'Word travels faster than lightning in this place.'

'Well, if Baba likes the prince so much, he can marry him,' Jasmine grumbled.

'Oh hush. He is very pretty,' Lina said dreamily.

'Then *you* can marry him,' Jasmine snapped, throwing herself on the bed.

'Oh dear, life is so hard for a princess with so many handsome men vying for her attention,' Lina said, sarcasm dripping from her words.

Jasmine glared at her.

'What? I'm just a handmaid, while *you* have the dashing Prince Ali and the dark and tantalising Jafar after you, even after you rejected all those other princes. Really, what is it that you want in a man?'

Jasmine sighed. What did she want in a man? Jafar's face came to mind, his intensity, his passion, the way it felt when he touched her. He never treated her like a trinket, as if she was a pretty face and good for nothing else. She never quite seemed to know what was going on in his mind, and that both frustrated and intrigued her.

'Maybe what I want is not to need a man at all,' she said, because it seemed like the most sensible answer. It seemed like the most sensible *option*. Prince Ali was respectable, she supposed, and she was supposed to marry a prince. Jafar, on the other hand, gave her what she didn't know she'd needed, but just as quickly took it away. What was it that made him so hot and cold?

'Well, you might want to choose someone before your father chooses for you. After all, he's been very lenient with you. Not many in his position would give you so much choice,' Lina said.

'What do you want in a man?' Jasmine asked suddenly, she'd never thought to ask. Was what she wanted really so wrong?

'Why do you want to know?' Lina asked sceptically, an eyebrow raised.

'Why don't you want to tell me?' Jasmine persisted, her curiosity piqued by Lina's reluctance to speak.

Lina sighed. But as she opened her mouth, a knock sounded at the door. They both turned to look at it, wondering who would be visiting at this time of night. For a moment she wondered if it was Jafar standing outside her door, come to sweep her up in another moment of passion, to apologise for staying away and ignoring her. She would forgive him, if only he would promise never to do it again.

Could she find happiness with him? A love like her mother and father had?

But when Lina opened the door, it wasn't Jafar standing there. It was Prince Ali, a bashful expression on his face as he raked his hand through his hair. Lina turned to her, eyebrows jumping to her hairline as she stepped away, finding something to busy herself with in the bathroom.

'Prince Ali, what an inappropriate surprise,' Jasmine said as she moved towards the door her handmaid had so helpfully vacated.

'I didn't know you were such a stickler for the rules, princess,' Ali said, flashing her a smirk that stirred a sense of familiarity in her. Had they met before? Surely she would have remembered him if they'd met. There was something about him that was different to all the other entitled princes she'd met, and yet that arrogance was still present.

'Oh? And what is it you think you know about me?' she challenged.

'Maybe I could get to know you. Would you take a stroll with me? I've heard the gardens here are the best in the land,' he said smoothly.

He was good, she'd give him that much. 'Yes, father is very proud of them. My mother loved the gardens.'

'So he maintains them for her? That's a marvellous gesture. I wonder what it must be like to love someone like that. Will you show them to me?'

Jasmine looked over her shoulder, trying to find an excuse to decline. Lina was nowhere to be seen. Traitor.

'Don't tell me you're afraid to break the rules,' he said, mischief shining in his eyes. It stirred another wave of familiarity, but more than that, it sounded like a challenge. She wasn't one to back down from a challenge.

'Fine,' she said grudgingly. She stepped outside the room and closed the door behind her. She could just imagine the grin on Lina's face. He offered her his arm, but she didn't take it, instead striding ahead of him, leading the way to the gardens.

Under the moonlight, the gardens didn't look like much, it was in the daylight when the flowers burst from the deep green leaves with vibrant colours, attracting the butterflies and the bees. Birds would sing in the trees and the sound of the water in the fountain seemed to chase the heat away. But under the cover of night it felt cool and colourless, the water was serene but Prince Ali was not who she wanted to enjoy it with.

As if he'd read her mind, he said, 'This place must be really something in the sunlight.'

'Yes,' Jasmine said absently. 'So, tell me about yourself, Prince Ali.'

He shrugged. 'What would you like to know?'

She could see this conversation wasn't going to get very far. He'd basically announced that there wasn't anything to know, nothing of particular interest. He took her hand in his, and that familiarity niggled at her again. That smirk, that mischief in his eyes, the way he grabbed her hand and led her through the gardens to the fountain, it was as if Aladdin was here with her, not Prince Ali.

As if her memory had suddenly cleared of a fog, she pulled her hand from his. Whoever he was, it was entirely inappropriate. He smiled sheepishly at her, muttering an apology.

If he was Aladdin, what did that mean? Was he a prince or a thief? What had he been doing in the marketplace if he was a prince? What was he doing in the palace if he was a thief? He had all the trimmings and the servants to suggest there was nothing false about his station, and the lineage.

'Princess?' he said, interrupting her thoughts with a quizzical gaze.

It was only then that she realised he'd been speaking to her. 'Sorry, what were you saying?'

'You don't like me very much, do you?' he asked.

She let out a sigh. 'I'm sorry, it's not you it's...I've spent my whole life couped up in one place or another. When my mother died, my father sent me away and now that I'm back all he wants to do is marry me off.'

'I'm sure the sultan just wants you to be safe, after what happened to your mother. He must be afraid of losing you, too.'

'I know. But I'm more capable than he thinks. I could run this kingdom, I don't need a husband to do that.'

'You want someone to rule beside you, rather than over you,' he said.

Her eyes widened in surprise. She hadn't expected that kind of understanding from him, he seemed frivolous and self-centred like the others. Maybe he was, but maybe there was also something more there. 'Have we met somewhere before? You just seem really familiar,' she said.

He chuckled awkwardly, raking his hand through his hair again. 'I don't think so. I'd definitely remember meeting you.'

He was smooth, and very good at deflecting, but she didn't quite believe him. Still, she wasn't going to push it yet, she would simply need to keep an eye on him. Was Lina right? Maybe this one wouldn't be so bad, but she didn't like not knowing his motives. Would he reveal those motives if she pushed him, if she played hard to get? In her experience, men seldom knew what to do when they were met with resistance from a woman. Would he slip up and let her know what he was hiding?

Would that work on Jafar?

'I should head back,' she said, making her decision. In part because she was trying to play hard to get and in part because Jafar seemed to consume her every thought as soon as he entered her mind. It was Jafar she wanted to be in the garden with, not Prince Ali. If he were here with her, would he kiss her as he had done the last time?

'I can't convince you to stay a while longer?' Prince Ali asked, taking her hand in his as he gazed into her eyes. He seemed well rehearsed in the art of seduction, she wondered how many times he had done this before.

'Not this time,' she said, making her tone flirtatious. Was it cruel to give him hope when she wasn't sure there was any? Maybe. But then, she wasn't entirely sure that Prince Ali wouldn't succeed. Her father liked him a little too well, he might just force her hand. 'Good night,' she said, slipping her hand from his grasp. She sauntered back to the palace, leaving him behind without so much as a backward glance. If he wanted to win her throne, she was going to make him work for it.

She rounded the corner and climbed a flight of stairs, grateful that she was finally getting her bearings around her own home again. Before she got her footing at the top, a hand clamped around her arm, pulling her into a dark corridor. She opened her mouth to protest, to call for the guards but another hand silenced her, muffling her voice. She was shoved against a wall, finally facing her attacker, coming face to face with Jafar's eyes, anger flashing through them like a storm as they bored into hers.

Her brow furrowed and she struggled against his grip, but he held her firmly, only releasing his hand from her mouth when she stilled. 'What the hell are you doing?' she demanded, keeping her voice low lest he gag her again.

'What am *I* doing? What are *you* doing, princess?' he hissed, his warm breath grazing her skin, making her heart race in her chest in a way it most definitely should not be in that moment.

What had gotten him so riled up, so furious with her? Had he seen her in the gardens with Prince Ali? She wasn't doing anything she shouldn't, in fact, for the first time she was actually doing what her father would have wanted.

Wait. Was he jealous? He'd kissed her so intensely in the garden and then he'd ignored her, as if he was pretending she didn't exist at all. But now he seemed so unlike the buttoned-up man who never showed his emotions, that nothing ever seemed to affect. Now he was raw and emotional and almost wild. Had she been the cause of it?

She held herself a little taller, confidence building within her. 'What is it that you didn't like, Jafar?' she asked, meeting his stormy gaze defiantly. 'Is it that I accepted Prince Ali's invitation or that he had the courage to do what you could not?'

Something like lightning flashed in his eyes then, something that should have sent a shock of fear through her, but instead it was anticipation slithering down her spine as she waited for him to answer her challenge.

'Tell me, princess,' he murmured, his voice a low rumble that seemed to vibrate across her skin. 'Did he make your heart race when he touched you?' His finger glided along her jaw, trailing down her neck, his eyes never leaving hers, his lips curling when she shivered under his touch. He leaned in close, his lips hovered above hers. 'Did you want him to kiss you?'

Her breath hitched in her throat as the kiss from the garden flashed in her mind. She wanted his kiss, she wanted to taste him again. It took all her strength not to move, not to reach out for him and close that distance between them, the one he'd left there to torture her.

'What if I said yes?' she breathed, her eyes flicking back to his to gage his reaction.

'I'd call you a liar,' he said with a dark confidence that sparked a throbbing need between her legs. He took her lips in a searing kiss that burned her from the inside out, as she gasped at the intensity, at the desire he was building in her. He pressed himself against her, his hands sliding down her body, gripping her hips, pulling her to him. His lips trailed along her jaw, down her neck, and she curled her fingers in his hair, leaning into him, her body craving more. She cursed the restriction of her clothes as he reached the neckline of her dress, her aching nipples begging for his kiss. As if reading her thoughts, a growl rumbled in his chest.

For a moment she thought he would stop as he leaned his forehead against her chest, his breathing heavy, his hands gripping her skirt, and she bit her tongue to prevent herself from begging him not to. His hands seemed to tremble, slowly bunching the fabric, slowly lifting it higher as though of their own accord, as though he were willing himself to stop but he couldn't. The idea that she could make him lose control of himself like that had a wetness seeping into her underwear as her need for him intensified.

He sucked in a breath as he revealed her thighs and she sunk her teeth into her lip to keep from crying out at his touch, her head falling back as his hands climbed higher, higher, skirting along the edges of her underwear. Her hand slipped to his shoulders, gripping him as he slipped one finger inside the fabric, touching her bare flesh.

He looked at her as he shoved the fabric aside, his eyes dark with desire. 'Tell me, princess, does he make you wet for his touch?' he asked, his voice husky and low as his fingers slipped between her folds, brushing against her clitoris. She bit into her lip so hard that pain blossomed there, knowing that she couldn't make a sound or he would have to stop. He captured her lips again as he stroked her, stifling her moans with his kiss, and each muffled sound vibrating along their lips seemed to spur him on. She gripped him to steady herself, to keep from collapsing at his touch as a tightness began to build in her core.

He slipped a finger inside her and her legs buckled, her fingers digging into him. He used his other arm to hold her up as he continued his relentless pleasure. His lips dropped to her neck again, and she felt she would explode if she couldn't make a sound soon.

'Don't stop,' she begged, her voice breathy and wanton but she didn't care.

'Never,' he growled against her skin as he slipped a second finger inside her.

She barely kept herself from crying out as the dam broke in an explosion of pleasure that rippled through her body, her muscles quivering as she orgasmed on his fingers. He pulled them from her and she shuddered against him. He let her skirt fall back into place as their heavy breaths tangled together in the cover of darkness.

Finally, he released her, straightening himself up, a wicked glint in his eyes. 'Next time you're with him, I dare you not to think of me.' With that he stalked away, her gaze lingering long after he had disappeared from her sight.

Chapter 12

Jafar

Jafar slammed the door to his chambers so hard the wood splintered in protest. His emotions were boiling within him, each of them fighting for dominance. He paced the room, barely aware of his surroundings as he tried to reign them in long enough for sanity to reassert itself.

He'd seen her in the garden with Prince Ali. The boy might just have what it took to win her heart, with his boyish charm and the ease in which he took her hand, as if it was his to take. He had a smooth confidence about him that declared to all the world that she would soon be his.

That ugly feeling had stirred from its slumber in his chest, spreading through his veins until he couldn't think straight. He'd lost control in that moment, and unable to keep a lid on his jealous rage he'd waited for her in that corridor, he'd grabbed her and fucked her with his fingers as if she was his to claim.

And God, she'd *let* him.

He'd wanted revenge on her for tormenting him, he'd gone there hoping to get inside her head, to plague her thoughts, haunt her dreams, so why did it feel like she had more control over him than ever?

He swept his hands over the table, scattering the contents to the ground in a clutter of sound and shattering glass, tangled with his own roar of frustration. He'd spent most of his life working towards his goal, clawing his way to the top. He'd finally made it, only one step away from having everything he'd ever wanted, and she had rolled in like a storm set on his destruction.

What was it about this woman that devoured his sanity? He was supposed to *want* her to marry a prince and secure the kingdom, but instead he wanted to kill this pretentious prince for having the audacity to touch what was *his*.

His. As if he could lay claim to her, as if he *should*.

He needed to refocus, he needed to get his hands on that lamp. Then he could wish these feelings away and his life would return to normal.

Even as he thought it, he didn't know if he had the strength to make such a wish.

One way or another, this woman would be the death of him.

Jafar groaned as he opened his heavy eyelids, the steady light of the sun streaming in through the window he'd forgotten to close the night before. His head throbbed and his mouth felt dry. Once again, Princess Jasmine had been the cause of him indulging in too much wine in the hopes of dulling his feelings.

He pulled himself out of bed, knowing he needed to be present today, it would be suspicious if he wasn't and he would not leave Prince Ali free to woo the sultan and the princess. He needed to ensure the engagement didn't go ahead. This prince had lasted far too long. The sultan had pinned his last hope on the boy, and he couldn't figure out what it was about him that had Jasmine hesitating but he didn't like it.

'Good morning, master,' Iago said hesitantly, his eyes casting about the room and the scattered items Jafar had ignored in favour of his wine glass.

'What of the lamp?' Jafar asked, cutting to the chase. He needed it now more than ever, though he wasn't sure if he'd wish his feelings gone or for Jasmine to be his. Either way, it solved his most immediate problem. But first he had to get his hands on it.

'Uh...well, the thing is, the cave it...'

'Spit it out man,' Jafar snapped, his patience had well and truly dried up.

'It's gone, master,' Iago said, shrinking slightly as if he thought Jafar would strike him for being the bearer of bad news.

And he might have, if he hadn't been too stunned. 'It's gone?' he repeated. He'd sent many men in there over the past two years, and all of them had failed. He'd assumed they'd died though he'd never been able to check. Still, the cave had remained.

What was different this time?

This time Aladdin had retrieved the lamp, but Jafar had thrown him back in. If the fall hadn't killed him, could he have figured out what the lamp did? Prince Ali's face came to mind, that sense of familiarity he couldn't shake and yet still he couldn't place. When he tried to picture Aladdin's face to compare them, he couldn't seem to summon an image. Could they be one and the same?

'Set a spy on Prince Ali,' Jafar said, and Iago looked up at him, confusion etched on his face. 'I want to know anything unusual he does, I want to know of any...unusual items he might be keeping.'

Iago blinked rapidly as he processed this, but clearly decided not to risk asking questions. He nodded quickly and fled from the room to do his master's bidding.

For the first time since Prince Ali had arrived, Jafar felt a spark of hope. If Ali was in fact Aladdin, then he could expose him as the fraud he was. If he exposed him, then Princess Jasmine would be safe once more. He still couldn't have her, he wasn't a prince, but perhaps he could content himself with being her lover, provided no other man could touch her.

Would that be enough?

Yes, he thought, even as he knew he was lying to himself. He'd never been the kind of man who could settle for half a prize, who could settle for less than what he truly wanted. If he could not marry her, his jealousy would consume him, he'd spend his life half crazed for her.

He shook himself. One problem at a time. First he needed to rid himself of Prince Ali. Even if he wasn't Aladdin, his spy would surely turn up something he could use against the boy.

But how long would that take? Jafar looked at his sceptre. There was a faster way to get the information he desired. Ruby eyes glinted at him from the head of that golden snake. He'd read about the sceptre in a dust ridden scroll hidden at the very back to the library when he was a scribe's assistant. He'd figured all the very best things to know about would be hidden away.

The Serpentine Sceptre was considered dark magic, almost limitless in its abilities, though the power came with a price. It drained the user's energy. Use too much power and it could end your life. Many a man had lost his life to it, arrogantly thinking they would never go too far. But Jafar knew that power like that was addictive. Used sparingly, it wouldn't affect the user much at all, but the more it was used, the more addictive it became, like opium.

Jafar had used it on occasion to sway someone's mind to pass a vote or steer the country subtly in the right direction, or to deter those who plotted against him, though in all honesty, he found that his own wit was usually sufficient to deal with such things.

A little loss of energy was a small price to pay if it would rid him of Prince Ali.

Before he could talk himself out of it, Jafar grabbed the sceptre and headed towards Prince Ali's rooms. The prince was already walking down the corridor, his triumphant expression like claws in Jafar's flesh. To the boy's credit, the expression dropped from his face when he saw Jafar.

As if he felt that Jafar had wronged him in some way, there was a seething anger tucked away in his eyes that didn't manage to reach the rest of his features. Was this more proof or did his animosity stem from something else?

'Good morning, your highness,' Jafar said smoothly, though it grated on him. He hated treating this pompous brat with respect. No doubt the prince had done very little to deserve it, other than be born to the right family.

'Yes, and to you...sorry, I forget your name,' Prince Ali said, trying for nonchalance but Jafar noted a hint of hostility in his words.

Jafar cared little. He held his sceptre steady, ensuring the eyes of the snake were aimed at the prince. Ali looked at it, as if the shining gold of it had lured his attention, though Jafar knew that it was more than that. It was the sceptre's power drawing the prince's gaze, it was impossible for any man to resist. Jafar could feel the power building, but that entranced look didn't appear on Prince Ali's face.

Was it not working?

'Tell me, how are you progressing with the princess?' Jafar asked. It was not the question he wanted to ask, but he couldn't risk exposing himself if the sceptre wasn't working.

'Why should I tell you?' Prince Ali asked defensively, his eyes snapping away from the sceptre and back to Jafar.

Definitely not working. Strange. None had ever been able to resist the sceptre's magics before. Was it a sign that stronger magics were at play?

'I am the sultan's advisor,' Jafar said simply. 'We're all hoping for the best outcome for everyone.'

Prince Ali smirked, that triumphant expression returning. 'The princess seems to be receptive,' he said with a shrug.

Receptive? That ugly feeling clawed at Jafar's chest again. *Was she as receptive to you as she was while she was riding my fingers?* he wanted to sneer. But that would only ruin Princess Jasmine's reputation and have Jafar thrown from the palace. He wondered if he could simply kill this prince and have done with it.

'The sultan will be pleased to hear this,' Jafar said, hating how true those words were. He inclined his head to Prince Ali before stalking away.

One thing was for certain, the sooner Prince Ali was out of the palace, the better.

Chapter 13

Aladdin

Aladdin paced his room as the Djinn watched absently from a chair, clearly not interested in his problems in the slightest. Things were not going at all as Aladdin had planned. He couldn't understand why the princess was holding back. Sure, she didn't know who he was, but he had expected her to feel that same connection they'd shared in the Agrabah marketplace, maybe to feel a familiarity about him, something to tempt her closer. But here in the palace, she was aloof, watchful, as if she suspected everyone of having ulterior motives.

He supposed a life surrounded by the scheming nobility would do that to a person, but he'd really thought she'd see past all that with him. Though he supposed he was scheming in a way, but it was different. He had come here for her, not for some nefarious reasons that she needed to be on guard for.

Worst of all, Jafar seemed to have caught on far quicker than the princess had. His eyes always seemed to be on Aladdin, always watching, as if he was waiting for him to make a mistake. And his visit that morning was far too suspicious. Aladdin had been in the palace all of a day and already the advisor was sniffing around him, as if he knew something wasn't right. He clearly hadn't figured it out yet, thanks to the Djinn magic, but Aladdin would need to be careful around him. If he did make a mistake, he didn't doubt that the advisor would put an end to his plans before they had even begun.

But if Jafar had already figured out so much, why hadn't the princess?

Aladdin let out a frustrated sigh. 'I don't understand,' he muttered, stabbing his fingers through his hair. His life on the streets may not have been glamourous, but it was easy and uncomplicated. He'd never had to waste so much time thinking about *anything* before.

But there were definitely perks to living in the palace. Could he really go back to the streets after all this? He supposed with the Djinn, he wouldn't need to marry the princess to live like a king, but for the first time in his life, he wasn't willing to let go just yet. He'd never found anything he wanted to hold onto before. Was that what love was? Or what is something else?

It was all starting to give him a headache.

'You don't understand what?' the Djinn asked, his tone clearly bored as he reached for another grape. The only person this arrangement seemed to benefit was the Djinn. He spent the day lounging in Aladdin's rooms, eating all the finest foods, and Aladdin was sure he'd seen a maid sneak out before the sun rose that morning.

'I don't understand why this isn't working. Why isn't she...'

'Falling for your lies? Hm...I wonder,' the Djinn said, an amused smile curling his lips before he popped the grape in his mouth, munching happily on it.

'It's not all lies, I'm still me,' Aladdin protested. He was still the man she'd met at the marketplace, the one who had saved her from the guards. He was still the man she'd danced with in the square in the light of the fire.

'But you're not, are you? You're Prince Ali now, and Prince Ali is like all the others. She's under no illusions, boy. She knows that all the men her father has put before her want her throne, not her. Why should she think you're any different? Are you going to tell me you haven't thought about it? Being *sultan*?' the Djinn said.

'Of course I have, who wouldn't think about it when it's a real possibility?' Aladdin snapped. To be sultan would mean never being poor again, never having to beg or steal. Being sultan would mean having lines of people waiting to do his bidding, having his choice of any woman to take to his bed, never having anyone look down on him again. 'But I came here for her,' he insisted, as if he was reminding himself and not the Djinn.

'Did you?' the Djinn asked, that bored tone returning to his voice.

'Yes!'

The Djinn shrugged. 'Reasons change, as do people. Perhaps you came with some misguided notions on winning a woman's heart, but you can't tell me that the luxury of this life, the power almost within reach, hasn't skewed your ambitions.'

Aladdin found himself unable to answer, his mouth clamping shut. Sure, it would be nice to have all that, especially when he'd had nothing his whole life, but that didn't mean his feelings for the princess were any less real. Why couldn't he have it all? He had a Djinn on his side, he could have anything he wanted.

Provided he could win her love.

But he didn't need her love to win her hand. Love could come with time. All he needed now was her consent to marriage, all he needed was for her to like him enough to say yes. And if the sultan liked him, that would surely help. He'd won the old man over easily enough, and he could feel Jasmine wavering, as if she might really be contemplating him. He just had to stay his course and he was sure he would succeed.

He would need to be wary of Jafar, though. The man was a lot smarter than Aladdin had anticipated and he would ruin everything if Aladdin wasn't careful.

'I've seen that look before,' the Djinn said. 'Be careful how high you reach, boy, or your wings might just catch fire.'

Aladdin looked at the Djinn with a furrowed brow. He didn't understand half the things that came out of his mouth. The Djinn merely sighed with exasperation. 'Perhaps you'd like to make your second wish, *master*,' he said, sneering the last word.

Aladdin was getting tired of the Djinn's attitude towards him, as if he wasn't worthy of being the master of the lamp. The Djinn looked at him the same way everyone else had looked at him his whole life; just a good for nothing street rat who would die in the gutter with a sword in his gut from robbing the wrong man.

'Back in the lamp, Djinn,' he snapped.

The Djinn's face darkened. 'We had a deal, boy,' he growled.

'Yes, we did. But right now, I need some privacy,' Aladdin said, his temper flaring. 'Now get back in the lamp.'

The Djinn looked like he was going to say something but changed his mind. He merely shrugged and in a trail of blue smoke, he returned to his lamp. Aladdin let out a frustrated sigh. In the garden, Jasmine had let him take her hand, she'd almost recognised him, he was sure of it. But then she'd pulled away. What would he tell her if she figured out who he was? Would he be able to fool her? Perhaps, but how long would it last? He needed to move faster. He needed to marry her before it was too late, before anyone found out who or what he was. Once they were married it would be too late for anyone to remove him and he would be in line to be the next sultan.

So how to entice the princess? He needed something that would appeal to her. Something to get her to open up to him, to believe he was different to all the others who had been placed before her.

And he knew better than anyone what that was.

She longed to do what she couldn't, what she shouldn't. She longed for freedom and adventure. He'd seen the way her eyes had lit up when they ran from the guards, that exhilaration after she'd jumped that rooftop, he'd seen the fascination in her expression when he'd shown her the marketplace at night. He couldn't sneak her out of the palace, if he got caught that would put a swift end to his plans. It would have to be something inside the palace that came with enough risk, forbidden enough to pique her interest.

If he could achieve that, he would propose to her quickly, before she could decide not to accept him, his moment would come while she was hesitant. And if he did it in front of her father, it would make it even harder for her to turn him down.

Feeling more confident now that he had a plan in place, Aladdin put on his hat and walked from the room with a smile on his face, confident in the knowledge that he would soon have everything he deserved.

Chapter 14

Jasmine

Jasmine had been in a haze all day. When she'd finally found her way back to her room last night, Lina had left, for which she was incredibly grateful. She wasn't sure how she would have answered the questions that would surely be flying at her if she'd been there waiting for her. She certainly hadn't been in a position to hide anything, her cheeks flushed, her hair disarrayed, her clothes wrinkled. She wasn't sure Lina would be able to even guess at what had happened.

She'd wanted that passion, that intensity Jafar had shown her glimpses of before, but last night was something entirely different. She wanted to see it again, even though she knew it was wrong. She wanted to see him again.

She sat at her vanity mirror, staring into her reflection absently, barely noticing Lina flitting about in the background, straightening sheets, pulling out clothes, lips moving but no words reaching Jasmine's ears.

'Alright, that's it,' Lina said, throwing a dress on the bed and marching towards her. 'What's going on?'

'Hmm? What do you mean?' Jasmine asked, coming back to reality.

'You've been absent all day, where has your mind been?'

'Nowhere,' she said quickly, picking up a brush and running it through her hair, focusing on it as if the task required her full attention.

Lina placed her hands on her hips, her expression stern. She wasn't buying it for one second, and Jasmine knew she wouldn't let it go until she had answers. 'How was your stroll with Prince Ali?'

Jasmine let out a sigh. 'It was fine, I suppose. There's something about him that seems so familiar to me.'

'Oh? Is he winning your heart?' Lina asked, her eyes brightening with interest.

Jafar's face came to Jasmine's mind, those stormy eyes focused on her, sending a fresh shiver down her spine as her body recalled his touch. 'What if...'

'What if?' Lina asked, a hint of hesitation creeping into her expression as if she had guessed that the question wasn't going to have a happy answer.

'What if I wanted someone I shouldn't? Someone I would never be allowed to marry?' she asked, regretting the words as soon as they'd left her mouth, her heart stinging as if she'd sliced it.

'Are we talking tall, dark, and handsome or street thief?' Lina asked.

Jasmine threw the nearest bottle at Lina, who easily dodged the item and chuckled. 'You make it sound like I'm just stringing men along left and right,' she complained.

Lina shrugged, a knowing smile on her face. 'Perhaps you can speak with your father tomorrow. He might be more accepting than you think. Unless you're talking about the street thief, then he might just lock you up for fear you'd gone mad.'

Jasmine laughed before she could stop herself. That was one thing she loved about Lina, the girl could make her smile even when she felt she might never be happy again. Would her father really listen? He was fond of Jafar, she could see it in the way they interacted, almost as if Jafar was the son he'd never had.

But what if he didn't? What if speaking up meant Jafar would be sent away, lose his position? What if Jafar didn't want her for a wife? Then he'd be forced into a marriage he didn't want.

Just as a sigh bubbled up her throat, a knock at the door sounded. Somehow, she knew who it was before Lina even opened the door to Prince Ali's charming grin. Disappointment settled over her. She was reminded again how fond her father was of the prince. Would he slight him in favour of Jafar? She wasn't sure.

'Prince Ali, two nights in a row,' Lina said, mock disapproval in her voice. 'You will have her back at a reasonable time tonight, won't you?'

Prince Ali was speechless for a moment, no doubt remembering her hasty retreat the night before. And now she had no choice but to go with him or he might grow suspicious. 'Don't listen to her,' Jasmine said. 'She retired early last night. I think she didn't *want* to be here when I got back.'

His face relaxed a little, that easy charm returning to his features. 'Will you join me again, princess?'

He was persistent, she would give him that. And she had little choice now that Lina had hinted at the idea of another man. Perhaps he wasn't bright enough to catch on, but on the off chance he was, she had to pretend that she was at least a little receptive to his advances. She wasn't ready to reveal Jafar to anyone just yet.

She offered a warm smile to hide the emotions roiling inside her. 'Of course.' She let him lead her down to the gardens again, the moon barely a sliver in the sky, shrouding them in thick shadows. He seemed to be walking with purpose, a giddy excitement surrounding him. 'Where are you taking me?' she asked, after some moments of silence.

'You'll see,' he said vaguely, piquing her curiosity. Did he know what he was doing? Was he manipulating her or was he simply a mischievous boy getting into to something he shouldn't? It was hard to tell with him.

He brought her to the pond, a place her father liked to keep exotic fish, though he rarely spent time in that part of the garden anymore, not since her mother's death. The water looked almost black in the thin moonlight, and despite knowing perfectly well that there was nothing in there that could harm her, she felt a sense of fear at the idea of what might lay beneath that blackness.

Prince Ali began removing his clothes.

'What are you doing?' she demanded, appalled, intrigued. She'd never seen a man naked before. But she found that it wasn't Prince Ali's naked form that she wanted to look upon. She felt her cheeks grow warm.

But Prince Ali merely smiled up at her, mischief shining in his eyes. 'Come, live a little, princess,' he said. He removed the rest of his clothes, though she refused to look at him as he did, and jumped into the water with a splash that almost reached her on the shore. His head broke through the surface, and he sighed in contentment. 'Well?' he asked.

Jasmine chewed her bottom lip as she looked down at the water which now contained a very naked prince. He was asking her to strip naked in front of him and swim. What else would he be expecting to happen?

'I promise I won't touch you unless you ask me to,' he said, guessing her fear. After a moment, when it seemed she wouldn't go in, he added, 'Are you afraid?'

He was goading her. She knew he was. And it was working. How many times had she lamented her situation, being couped up in a cage with no excitement in her life? Now this prince offered her a new experience, one she was most definitely not allowed, and she hesitated.

She took a deep breath. 'Turn around,' she said. He smiled wide and quickly did as she asked. She waited a moment, making sure he wouldn't turn back, then she slowly began to undress, letting her clothes fall to the cold stones at her feet, her skin prickling as the evening air touched it, her eyes firmly on the prince as she did, bracing herself to cover her naked flesh should he not keep his word.

Finally, she stepped forward, nervous excitement bubbling in her stomach, the kind she hadn't felt since she was a child. She stepped into the water, a shock of cold against her warm skin. Prince Ali kept his word, remaining turned as she slowly submerged herself with each step, until the deep black water covered up to her collarbones.

'Okay,' she said tentatively, feeling both vulnerable and brave at the same time.

Prince Ali turned around and grinned at her. 'I knew you were my kind of princess.'

'Oh? And what kind of princess is that?'

'Bold, adventurous, willing to try new things. I bet you crave that excitement, don't you?' he said and for the first time, he made her heart skip a beat. 'Now tell me you're not having at least a little fun.' He swam around, keeping a careful distance from her, though she was sure he would be at her side in a moment if she indicated her consent.

She couldn't help smiling. His carefree attitude was contagious and she found that she *was* having a little fun. For the first time in a long time, the palace didn't seem quite so dull.

Her mind flashed back to the intensity in Jafar's eyes, that storm raging there when she had merely walked with Ali and he'd taken her hand. What would he do if he caught her like this?

She shook his face from her mind, trying to focus on the present. She still had that sense of familiarity about Prince Ali, and seeing him swim about completely carefree, that mischief twinkling in his eyes, she was almost sure now that he was Aladdin.

'Do you make a habit of breaking rules, Aladdin?' she asked innocently, while waiting with bated breath to finally learn the truth.

He laughed. 'Sure, what's more fun than a little rule breaking?' he said. Suddenly, he froze, his gaze falling on her in surprise. She raised an eyebrow at him. 'How long have you known?'

She smiled but decided not to answer. 'So, how does a thief enter the palace as a prince?'

'I'm not. A thief, I mean. I – I came to the city early. I wanted to see what it was really like so I made myself look like one of them,' he said so smoothly she almost believed him. Almost. But then, she had no reason not to. How could a thief possibly pass himself off as a prince?

'Well, you put me to shame. You saw more of the city in a few days than I've seen my whole life,' she said, offering him an out.

'It's not as if you had a choice, princess. It was admirable that you snuck out to see it at all,' he said, sympathy in his eyes.

'Maybe one day I'll be allowed to leave the palace and really see my kingdom,' she said. 'What's your kingdom like?'

'Oh, uh...I'm not really sure how to describe it. It's not so different from Agrabah, really. For some reason, I like it much better here,' he said, his gaze locked on her. Was he distracting her by flirting with her?

She began to shiver, the cold from the water seeping into her muscles. She was about to ask Ali to turn around so she could get out when she heard footsteps. She turned quickly, finding Jafar standing at the edge of the water, that storm flashing in his eyes, pure rage on his face. It was different to the jealousy she'd seen the night before, and a shiver of fear raced down her spine.

'What the *hell* is going on here?' he demanded.

Prince Ali was stammering behind her, but she couldn't take her eyes off Jafar as she sank a little lower in the water. But then she remembered that *she* was the princess. He was an advisor. What right did he have to make her cower before him?

'Get *out*!' he ordered, and Ali scrambled out of the water, picking his clothes off the ground, stepping into them quickly. He hesitated a moment, and Jasmine feared what Jafar might do to him if he didn't run, so she nodded at him, giving him permission to leave. He didn't need any further prompting, fleeing the scene without so much as a backward glance. She realised that Prince Ali was fun and carefree, but he was also a coward.

'How long were you watching?' she asked.

'Long enough,' he growled.

Jafar stood on the shore, his fury trained on her, perhaps designed to pin her in place or make her feel shame. But she would not bend before him. She stood straighter, her head high, her face defiant. She strode forward, the water slowly receding, showing more skin with each step, slipping down her breasts, revealing tight nipples. The fury began to recede from his eyes as they widened in surprise, though he couldn't seem to pull his gaze away.

She stood before him on the shore, her body completely naked, shining and wet, the cold covering her skin in goosebumps, hardening her nipples. 'Nothing more to say, Jafar?' she asked, her voice almost a purr. She'd never shown a man her body before, but Jafar's hungry gaze sent a thrill through her.

What will you do now, advisor? she wondered as memories of last night flooded her. She ran her tongue along her bottom lip and waited for him to make his move.

Chapter 15

Jafar

Jasmine stood before him, nothing but shadows covering her naked flesh, her wet skin prickled at the touch of the air, her nipples already tight little buds begging to be sucked. A confident expression settled on her face, almost as if she was daring him to do something. The idea that another man had been treated to the sight of her naked form bristled inside him, leading his mind to dangerous places, even though he knew the prince hadn't touched her, hadn't been able to see anything beneath the surface of the water.

Would she have shown Ali if he hadn't interrupted? Would she have let Ali touch her, hear her moan the way she had beneath his hands? His jaw clenched, a muscle ticking as he glowered at her.

'Nothing more to say, Jafar?' she asked, quirking a single eyebrow at him as water dripped down her soft skin, skin he longed to touch again. He realised he'd been following one of those drips with his eyes and quickly flicked them back to her face, but the damage was done, he could tell by the smirk sitting on her lips. She'd known exactly what he'd done, exactly what she was doing to him.

She had no idea that she was playing with fire.

He knew he shouldn't, but he couldn't think with her looking like that. What man could resist when the object of his obsession stood so temptingly before him, begging for his tongue? He pulled her to him roughly, his lips capturing her squeak of surprise as she collapsed into him, her breasts pressed against his chest, and he cursed the fabric that still separated them.

She melted into him, her arms snaking around his neck, fingers curling in his hair as she pressed herself hard against him. His hand slid over her curves, exploring her body as he hadn't been able to before, sliding down to rest on her plump arse. He squeezed hard and she moaned against him. How wet would she be for him? He was growing hard, his cock aching to be inside her, even as he knew he couldn't. He was flirting with danger as it was, if anyone caught them, he'd be thrown in the dungeon, lucky if they scraped him off the floor to let him die. If he took her virginity, he'd be tortured in ways he could scarcely imagine, and yet a small voice in his mind whispered, *worth it.*

'Jafar, I *need* you,' she breathed, her voice full of a desperate need that had pre-come soaking into his pants. He groaned, any doubts fleeing his mind with her one simple request. He scooped her up, carrying her to a bench obscured by plants. She gasped as he placed her down on the cold stone, but the look in her eyes was pure desire. He raked a hand over his face. If he had ever had a chance to turn back, it was gone now.

'I need to taste you,' he said, his voice so husky he barely recognised it.

'*Yes,*' she moaned, sending a thrill of pleasure through him, right to his cock. This was going to be torture. *Worth it*, that voice whispered again.

He slid to his knees at her feet, sliding his hands up her legs. She fidgeted impatiently under his touch, and he licked his lips as her breasts bounced with each movement, her hands sliding over her own skin, inching closer to that sensitive flesh. As much as he wanted to grab them, he wanted to see them in her hands more.

'Touch them,' he ordered roughly. At his command, she brought her hands to her breasts, sliding them over her skin, squeezing them with a moan as she arched her back. His cock pulsed painfully in his pants.

He pushed her legs apart, staring down at her like a man in the desert staring at an oasis, as if he would die if he didn't taste her. He leaned forward slowly, inching closer as she fondled her breasts. She was so wet for him, he could see her need. With one strong lick, the taste of her exploded on his tongue and she cried out, quickly clamping a hand over her mouth to muffle the sound.

So responsive.

'Quiet now, or I'll have to stop,' he teased, enjoying the way her hair flew around her as she shook her head adamantly, her hand still on her mouth.

As if he could stop now that he'd tasted her.

He kept his hands on her thighs, fingers digging in to her flesh every time she tried to close them. She writhed on that stone bench, her free hand still at her breast, squeezing, pinching her nipple as his tongue darted out again and again, sliding through her folds, flicking her clitoris, dipping inside her. Her other hand muffled her moans, and God he wanted to hear her voice fill a room as he touched her. His cock pulsed with need. He wanted to stroke himself as he licked her. He wanted to feel her soft hands on him.

Her hand slid from her breast, slowly gliding down her stomach. For a moment he thought she was going to touch herself and he groaned against her sensitive flesh. Instead, her fingers curled in his hair and she pulled him to her. He could sense she was close and he licked at her with more fervour, desperate to taste her as she orgasmed on his tongue.

Her grip tightened, her body growing stiff, with a final flick of his tongue, he sent her careening over the edge. She screamed into her hand, her body shuddering as her orgasm rocked through her. He lapped at her, unwilling to let her go, savouring the taste of her. Her hand began pushing him away but he growled, determined to rend every last shudder from her.

Her hand fell away from her mouth, her body began to still, and she whimpered as he stroked her one final time with his tongue before he finally released her. He wanted to take her back to his room, to lock her in there for days, filling the hours with pleasure, learning every inch of her body, every reaction. His heart ached when logic reasserted itself, reminding him that he could never have her like that.

'Why do you look sad?' she asked, propping herself on her elbows.

Maybe he couldn't have that, but he could have this, just a little longer. Until he escorted her back to her room. Then he would say goodbye.

He kissed the inside of her thigh before rising to his feet to retrieve her clothes. He handed them to her, his fingers trailing along her skin absently as he gazed down at her. 'You should dress before someone sees,' he said. Her brow began to furrow at his words and he knew she'd taken them wrong, knew he should let her take them wrong, but for some reason he couldn't. 'I don't want anyone else to see you like this. I'm not big on sharing,' he said, his voice low. He captured her lips in a hungry kiss. She didn't know the half of it, if anyone saw her right now, he might just have to kill them.

She smiled gently at him, a smile she had never given him before, and slipped on her clothes. How was he ever going to let her go?

Jafar had barely been able to take her all the way to her door last night, and now he was forced to watch her with Prince Ali, the man who had talked her out of her clothes in the middle of the night. They were seated a respectable space away from each other, playing some kind of card game Jafar had no interest in. Each time she laughed, his molars ground together harshly. Every now and then she would cast her eyes to him, and every time he had to force himself to look away. No one could know what they had done, what *he* had done.

He was reminded once again that he could not have her.

Prince Ali had an easy smile on his face, clearly none the wiser that he didn't have her full attention. He laughed with her, casting her lust-filled looks every now and then, as if he were imagining what had been hidden beneath the water last night.

'Prince Ali and Jasmine seem to be getting on rather well, don't you think?' the sultan said happily, completely unaware of the turmoil raging inside Jafar.

'Indeed, your majesty,' he said.

'Prince Ali has spoken to me, you know. He wants to propose to Jasmine, he wanted my opinion on the matter. I'm quite fond of the lad, I believe he would make her a fine husband.'

'And if she refuses?' Jafar asked, his heart in his throat. He could feel the colour draining from his face, his lungs constricting as if he couldn't get enough air.

'I fear she might, but only because she is stubborn. If she refuses him, I will not feel guilty for forcing the issue. Look how well she likes him,' the sultan said, and as if on cue, Jasmine laughed, the sound cutting him worse than any blade. 'She will forgive me once she is happily married.'

'Indeed, your majesty,' Jafar bit out. The sultan looked over at him, an eyebrow raised in question. Jafar cleared his throat. 'Forgive me, your majesty, I have other things on my mind.'

The sultan nodded in understanding, even though Jafar knew the man had no idea. He assumed Jafar was thinking of matters of state, which was for the best. 'I'll not keep you from your duty,' the sultan said. 'I think things will be quiet this afternoon.'

He was being dismissed. He wasn't sure what was worse; watching Prince Ali attempting to woo Jasmine or not being there to watch it. But there was nothing he could do about it now. He bowed to the sultan, then strode towards the door. He could feel her eyes on him and he forced himself not to turn around. He couldn't allow himself to look back at her, not with the sultan watching.

He felt agitated, clenching and unclenching his fist as he walked, fighting the urge to storm back into the room and throw the princess over his shoulder. He needed something to focus on, something to take his mind off her.

He needed to hit something.

'Master,' Iago called after him, seemingly breathless as if he had run around the palace in search of him. When he caught up, he bent over, hands on his knees, breathing hard as Jafar looked at him with a raised eyebrow. 'Master, there is news,' Iago said once he had finally caught his breath, unaware that he was trying his master's patience. His voice was low, conspiratorial.

'Well, what is it?' Jafar asked irritably. He was in no mood to gently coax the answer from the man. Though, Iago should be used to that. There wasn't much about Jafar that could be considered gentle.

'It's about,' he said, pausing to look around the empty corridor as if he suspected someone might be listening. Jafar barely resisted the urge to sigh. 'Prince Ali.'

'What of him?' Jafar asked, his body tensing in anticipation. Was this it? Was he finally going to get rid of that thorn in his side?

'He has the lamp.'

Prince Ali had the lamp. That could only mean one thing; Prince Ali was in fact the street rat Aladdin.

A smile spread across Jafar's lips and he could tell it was as vindictive as he felt because Iago flinched and gazed down at his feet. 'Well done, Iago,' he said, and the man's eyes widened in surprise before a happy smile appeared on his face. He bowed and scurried away.

Jafar would need to take the lamp from Aladdin, and in so doing, he could out him as the fraud he was. He would no longer be a threat. Things were finally going his way.

Chapter 16

Jasmine

J asmine had finally been released from her activities with Prince Ali. It wasn't that she hadn't enjoyed their time together, but there was a shadow hanging over it. Jafar had been present in the beginning. He had spent most of the time scowling, and whenever she caught his eyes he would look away. She couldn't understand why he would ignore her after what they'd done last night. A shiver ran down her spine at the memory, her skin prickling. He'd been so passionate, but something like despair had swept over him, though he wouldn't admit to it.

Why was he ignoring her now?

It wasn't as if she could demand answers from him in front of everyone. She'd hoped to get him alone, but her father had dismissed him before she'd had the chance. He hadn't even glanced at her as he'd left, and she was surprised how much it made her heart ache.

'You look utterly miserable,' Lina said as she brushed Jasmine's hair.

'I don't think I will ever understand men,' Jasmine lamented. 'They are so contradictory. One minute they make you feel like the most important thing in the world, the next they're acting like you don't even exist.'

Lina tilted her head at Jasmine's reflection. 'Well, now I know we're not talking about Prince Ali. He wouldn't *dream* of sending you mixed messages. So, that means we're talking about Jafar.' She wiggled her eyebrows conspiratorially, eliciting a giggle from the princess. 'Well, as much as I *hate* delving into the dark shadows in the minds of men, I will do it for you. But I need to know what happened.'

'You're terrible. Bribing me to tell you my secrets,' Jasmine teased.

Lina hiked a shoulder innocently. 'Spill.'

'You can't tell anyone,' Jasmine said, her stomach fluttering nervously. Lina just looked at her as if she was an idiot, which was probably fair, but she'd never done anything like that before. She wondered what Lina would think of her. Would she be appalled? Disgusted that a princess would do something so wicked? Horrified that she wanted to do it again?

Jasmine took a deep breath. 'Last night when I was with Prince Ali, we went to the pond. Jafar caught us there –'

'Caught you doing what? I feel like I'm missing the best part of the story.'

Jasmine glared at her. 'We were...swimming.'

Lina's eyes widened and she waved Jasmine on, an excited expression on her face that made Jasmine's stomach flutter more, a blush beginning to rise to her cheeks.

'He sent Prince Ali scurrying away. He looked furious and I – it doesn't matter. He kissed me again and he...' Jasmine trailed off, blushing furiously.

'He what? What did he do?' Lina asked as if she couldn't bear the suspense any longer.

'He, uh...kissed me... somewhere else...'

Lina's eyes widened. 'He did *that* in the garden for anyone to see?'

'I mean, he did sort of hide us from view,' Jasmine muttered but Lina was too busy fanning herself to pay attention. 'But today he wouldn't even look at me.'

Lina stopped abruptly, her face suddenly turning serious. 'He doesn't strike me as the kind of man to do something like that lightly. He's also not a prince.'

'And?'

'And therefore he can't marry you,' Lina said as if it were the most obvious thing in the world. And to be fair, it really was. Jasmine knew there was a stipulation around her marrying a prince, but she supposed deep down she'd hoped it could be overlooked. Her father was fond of Jafar and he could help her run the country far better than any prince. 'He's probably trying *so* hard to keep away from you, but his passions can't be denied!' Lina said dramatically, fanning herself again.

'Don't be ridiculous,' Jasmine said, rolling her eyes. But what if she was right? Was his status a bigger hurdle than she'd ever realised? To her it seemed ridiculous, a thing that could easily be overturned with one word from her father, but to Jafar it might seem like an insurmountable obstacle. 'So you're saying whatever this thing is between us, it's doomed?'

Lina smacked her on the arm. 'Hush, I said no such thing! He just needs to be convinced to fight for you.'

'How do I do that?' Jasmine asked.

Lina sifted through the wardrobe quickly and pulled out a dress made of thin white fabric, sheer enough to see the outlines of her body, enough to make it tantalising. It was a piece of clothing that was in her wardrobe in preparation for her marriage, something she was supposed to wear for her husband. Jasmine raised her eyebrow at her handmaid.

'You wear this and you go to his chambers. When you're there, you'll take him in your hand, or your mouth, if you're feeling adventurous.'

'In my...' Her mind wandered back to the garden, how he'd taken her with his mouth. What would it be like to return the favour? What would he do if she did? Her cheeks flushed again.

'Trust me, men love that. I dare him to ignore you after that,' Lina said confidently, a wicked glint to her eye that was contagious.

Yes, she would go to him and she would dare him to ignore her after this.

It had seemed like a good idea while Lina was bolstering her courage, but now that she had her bare feet on the palace floor, the cold stone creeping into her skin, she was having second thoughts. She pulled her cloak tighter around herself and took a deep breath. She had to do this. She was sick of Jafar ignoring her after igniting these feelings in her. He was going to learn that she would not be ignored.

She slipped through the palace, grateful for the cover of darkness, avoiding all the guards as she went. It would make little difference if she was seen, they couldn't exactly stop her or even ask where she was going, but she was afraid that someone else might find out, someone who *could* ask questions.

Each step made her feel bolder, and she was sure that was due to the absinth Lina had forced her to drink before she'd shooed her out the door. 'For luck,' she'd said with a wink, but Jasmine now suspected that it was to keep her from changing her mind.

She reached Jafar's door, a place she had never been before, and her stomach gripped tightly. What if Lina was wrong?

She took a deep breath and forced herself to knock. As soon as the sound rang out through the corridor, she regretted it; there was no turning back now. The seconds ticked by like an eternity and her stomach knotted with anxiety. She heard movement inside and was tempted to run, but instead she squared her shoulders and stood tall, feigning a confidence she didn't feel.

The door was pulled open and Jafar stood in the way, a scowl on his face which quickly dissolved into a look of surprise. 'Princess, is something wrong?' he asked. She could see his mind scrambling to make sense of her presence and she liked the feeling of being one step ahead of him.

'Do you really want to know?' she asked, looking up at him with hooded eyes. Before he could answer, she slipped past him into the room, looking around her. It was lit dimly by a single candle burning low on his desk. Papers were littered across it and she was surprised for a moment that he'd been working this late into the night, though she realised she shouldn't be. He'd always been that way. Aside from his desk, the rest of the room was perfectly orderly, not a thing seemed out of place. It seemed he was meticulous with every aspect of his life, and that only made her want to ruffle him even more.

'Princess –' Jafar began, something like a warning in his voice, but a half-hearted one, one she suspected he didn't want her to heed.

'Are you going to keep calling me that?' she asked. She dropped her voice, giving it a sultry air. 'Even when we're alone?'

His brows furrowed and he refused to move, as if he had been rooted to the floor, the door still ajar. 'What are you doing?'

She walked towards him, closing the distance between them, aware that if anyone happened by it would require an awful lot of explaining. For some reason, she couldn't seem to bring herself to care. 'What do you want me to do?' she asked, bringing her hand to his chest.

His hand shot out, clamping around her wrist to stop her. 'You shouldn't be here.'

She slipped her hand from his grip, surprised at how easily he let go. She could leave now and admit defeat, but she'd come this far, and she could see the hesitation in his eyes. 'Oh? Are you telling me to leave?' she asked, pouting. She turned from him and unclasped her cloak, letting it flutter to the floor, revealing her dress. She looked over her shoulder at him, his eyes had widened and he raked a hand over his mouth. There was a hunger in his eyes that was undeniable. He wanted this as much as she did.

He just needs to be convinced to fight for you.

'Aren't you at least a little curious?' she asked. She let her gaze travel down his body as she imagined what he hid beneath those robes. When she looked back to his eyes, the hunger had intensified. 'Close the door, darling,' she said softly, her lips curling sensually as anticipation began to flutter in her stomach.

As if in a trance, he pushed the door and she waited until she heard the click before she began sauntering towards him. She tried to put her anxieties aside, to keep her confident façade showing, even as questions flooded her mind. She'd never tried to seduce a man before, she'd never done the things she was about to do. What if she was bad at it? What if he didn't like it?

She focused on the words Lina had told her as she'd shot the burning spirit down her throat. *Confidence is sexy, and when you get there, just focus on feeling. Don't be afraid to be curious about him, men love that.*

Would you love that, Jafar? she wondered as she reached up, touching one finger to his chest, watching it trail down the dark fabric covering his body. She was curious. She wanted to know what he looked like beneath the clothes, she wanted to know what he would feel like in her hand, in her mouth. How would he taste?

'Why have you come, princess?' he asked, his voice husky.

Jasmine clicked her tongue in irritation. She was going to have to force him to lose that title if she was going to convince him to fight for her, for *them*. She pushed up onto her toes, bringing her face close to his. She flicked her tongue across his lips, resisting the urge to smile as his breath hitched. She looked up at him, her gaze steady. 'Not princess.'

He hesitated, his eyes searching hers. She lowered herself back to her feet, an eyebrow arched as she waited. 'Why have you come, Jasmine?'

Hearing her name on his lips made her toes curl. She never wanted to hear the word *princess* from him again. She smiled up at him, then pressed her lips to his, rewarding him for his good behaviour. She slid her hands up his chest as his arm snaked around her waist and he groaned in ecstasy. She could feel his erection growing as her body pressed against his. His hands slid over the sheer silk of her dress, and she wondered if he imagined ripping it from her, exposing her body to him as she had in the garden.

His hand slid up her back, his skin hot, making her shiver with pleasure. She felt that curiosity again and she followed it, slipping her tongue between his lips, stroking his own. As if she'd spurred him, his grip tightened, pulling her tighter to him, his lips devouring hers hungrily, deepening the kiss, leaving her breathless.

She was losing herself in him and she forced herself to break away. She wasn't going to let him take control this time. Tonight, she was going to take control. She looked up at him, enjoying the look of confusion on his face, her finger lingering on his robes. 'Won't you take it off?' she asked.

'You truly are untameable,' he said, though it didn't sound as if he disapproved.

She smiled wickedly. 'But it would be fun to try.' Though tonight she hoped he wouldn't try, not yet. There were things *she* wanted to try first.

Chapter 17

Jafar

J asmine stood before him, a sheer white silk dusting her skin, offering him glimpses of her silhouette beneath, a tantalising reminder of her naked body laid out before him in the garden, and now she was in his room, that sultry lilt to her voice, lust colouring her cheeks the most delicious shade of pink, desire dancing in her eyes. Desire for him.

When she'd ordered him to close the door, calling him *darling*, his body had moved on its own. He was powerless to resist her. She was wearing the gown that was meant for her husband, wearing it for him, a man who could never be that for her. Anger and desire warred within him. He never wanted another man to see her dressed like that.

Now she was looking up at him, asking him to take off his clothes. His cock twitched at her request. He'd dreamed about being inside her since she'd come on his tongue, dreamed of her coming on his cock. It would be all too easy to get carried away with her here in his room. He couldn't take her, not that way. Not ever.

Not yet, a treacherous voice whispered in the back of his mind.

'No,' he managed to bite out, the word scraping along his tongue like a razor. He so badly wanted to give into her, to get swept up in her. But if he did, it would jeopardise everything he'd worked so hard for.

She pouted. 'Won't you let me explore you like you explored me?' she asked, her gaze holding his as her hand slipped down his chest, making its way lower, lower, inching towards his aching cock. He couldn't pull his eyes away as he waited, anticipation for her touch coiling in him. She grazed her hand over his erection and a groan rumbled in his chest, his eyelids growing heaving. God, he had dreamed of her touch, and it was nothing compared to the reality of it.

He clasped a hand around her wrist, stilling her, but he could tell from the look on her face that he hadn't deterred her. 'You don't know what you're starting, princess,' he said, trying to cling to his last thread of sanity.

She held his gaze steadily, that unshakable confidence clinging to her as it always had. 'I know exactly what I'm starting,' she said. 'And if you refuse to say my name, I'll have you screaming it before the night is out,' she challenged, a flicker of heat darting through her eyes.

'Strong words, *princess*,' he said, his voice betraying the lust she'd ignited in him.

Still holding his gaze, she rubbed her free hand over his cock, a slow and confident stroke that made him shudder with need. His hips bucked against her hand and a slow smile crept across her lips, a triumphant smile.

God, this woman was going to be the death of him.

'Don't you want to feel my hand on you? The heat of my skin as I grip you?' she purred.

He did want that, more than anything now that she'd voiced it. The idea sounded so enticing coming from her lips in that lust filled voice, as if she wanted it as much as he did. Her eyes dropped to his erection and her tongue darted out to lick her lips. That was it, he was gone, his restraint shattered.

His clothes were on the floor before he realised he was complying, and that wicked smile stretched lazily across her lips again. She could have her fun for now, but she would be at *his* mercy before the night was out. He reached out for her but she placed her hand on his chest to stop him. What was that look in her eyes? Something mischievous, something dangerous.

When she seemed satisfied he wouldn't move, she slid her hands over his skin, feeling the muscles beneath, hovering over scars, as if she was committing his body to memory. She brushed a kiss over one and goosebumps raced across his skin. She seemed to like that reaction and she brushed a kiss to another. She was taking her time, not only learning his body, but learning his reactions, what he liked, as if she had come with the intention to please him. He stifled a groan at the thought, his cock pulsing painfully with need.

As if she'd noticed, she slid her hand slowly down his torso, having no idea how torturous her slow touch was. Or maybe she did. That wicked glint was in her eyes again. He was going to punish her for that later.

Another groan escaped him when she wrapped her hand around his cock, and her smooth, warm skin against his felt better than he ever imagined. She studied his reaction before sliding her palm up his shaft, then back down again in a painfully slow motion. She did it again, faster this time, and his head fell back as pleasure shot through him.

He wanted to reach out for her, to fist his hand in her hair and kiss her hard as she stroked him. Would she let him? What if she stopped? The little witch might just do it, she seemed intent on controlling this. How long could he last? He had never been the kind of man to relinquish control to anyone.

She pumped her fist again, he couldn't take it anymore. He reached out for her, his fingers grazing her hair before she stopped and stepped away. He barely suppressed a growl of frustration. She moved towards the bed, hooking her finger at him, bidding him to follow as if she expected him to do exactly what he was told like a good little boy.

She would learn the difference between playing with a boy and playing with a man this night.

He strode after her, intending to rip that dress from her before taking her lips, her breasts, and any other part of her he desired. But she took a pillow from the bed. 'Sit,' she said, her voice breathy, a look of anticipation in her eyes. His mind raced to catch up to hers, to figure out what she intended. When he didn't move, she dropped the pillow on the floor and raised an eyebrow in challenge.

Could she really mean...?

'Are you going to keep me waiting?' she asked. Her tongue ran along her lip again and his body began moving of its own accord. He stood inches from her, his heart pounding in his chest, anticipation coiled so tightly he needed release. But he needed more than her mouth, he wanted every inch of her.

'Take this off,' he said, bunching the fabric in his hand.

'Sit,' she said again.

Infuriating woman. If she was his, he would tear it from her body. He'd pin her to the bed, her hands above her head as he took her nipple in his mouth. But she wasn't his.

Not yet.

He clenched his teeth, a muscle ticking in his jaw as he did as she instructed, sitting on the bed. She smiled at him, his reward for doing as he was told, and that muscle ticked again. When she was his, he was going to punish – she slipped her dress from her shoulders, letting it fall to the floor, revealing her body to him once more. In the dim candlelight he could appreciate it better; her smooth golden skin, the curve of her hips, those plump breast with jutting nipples just begging to be sucked.

'Let me touch you, princess,' he said, a hint of desperation to his voice that he resented.

'No,' she said triumphantly. His hands balled into fists at his side as he tried to restrain himself. She moved towards him, standing between his legs before sliding down to her knees. Her breasts brushed over his cock and it pulsed, the head growing slick as he bit back a groan.

When she settled, she looked at his length and her tongue darted across her lips again. If she didn't stop doing that, he wasn't going to be held responsible for his actions. A flicker of uncertainty darted across her face and he was reminded that she had likely never done anything like this before, despite her bravado.

She had better not have done anything like this before.

He was about to change the game, not wanting her to do anything she didn't want to but not willing to release her yet, when she gripped his shaft in her hand and leaned in.

She licked her tongue over his swollen head and he hissed in a breath.

As if encouraged by his reaction, she ran her tongue along the length of his shaft, flicking it over the head again. Then she wrapped her lips around the engorged tip. His head nearly fell back as pleasure pulsed through him, but he forced himself to resist, he wanted to watch this. His hands clenched tighter as she slid him deeper, slowly deeper. Watching his cock disappear into her mouth was the most erotic thing he'd ever seen. When she pulled back, she followed her mouth with her hand.

'Ah, God, that's it,' he moaned.

The wicked creature met his gaze, holding it as she flicked her tongue again. He knew he wasn't going to last long, he gripped the sheets tighter, trying to hold out a little longer as she descended again, sucking him deep, pumping her hand. He groaned, his head falling back. A part of him didn't want to tell her, wanting her to swallow his seed. Ah, hell, he couldn't do that to her.

He looked down at her. 'Princess, I'm going to –' he forced the words out.

She looked up at him, a fire flashing in her eyes. *If you refuse to say my name, I'll have you screaming it before the night is out*, her words came back to his mind as she took him deeper. She knew what he was going to say, knew what was coming, she wanted it.

'Jasmine,' he groaned as he curled his hand in her hair, his head falling back once more, unable to fight the ecstasy building within him. So close. It was as if his deepest fantasies were coming true. With that thought, a guttural growl ripped from his chest as his orgasm rocked through

him. She greedily sucked at him, swallowing every drop before releasing him from her mouth as he let her hair slip between his fingers, his arm falling back to the mattress.

She leaned back on her knees, running her thumb along the corner of her mouth, a triumphant smile on her perfect lips, her cheeks flushed with desire. She was without a doubt the most beautiful creature he'd ever beheld, and she wanted *him*. Could they have this? If he tried, could he have her? Whether it was possible or not, he knew one thing for certain; he wasn't letting her go just yet.

He leaned forward, running his fingers along her arm before taking her hand and helping her to stand. He wanted to bring her to him, wanted her to straddle him, wanted to feed his cock inside her, to watch her breasts bounce as she rode him. But he couldn't have that.

Not yet.

He stood then, one arm snaking around her waist, roughly pulling her to him, taking her lips with a groan as her breasts pressed against his chest, soft and plump against his hard muscles. He turned with her in his arms, then pushed her back onto the mattress. She looked up at him, a bewildered excitement in her eyes.

'It's my turn now,' he said, taking her place on the pillow, his eyes already on the apex of her thighs. He pushed her knees apart so he could fit between them but she resisted him. He looked up at her, frustration warring with confusion.

'You don't have to,' she said, a blush rising to her cheeks. 'I came to please you.'

'This pleases me,' he growled, pushing her knees apart. He leaned forward, giving her pussy a strong lick. She moaned, collapsing back to the mattress, the resistance she'd attempted crumbling, her legs falling open for him. His hands slid up her thighs, curling around her hips. He pulled her to his mouth as he licked, his tongue flicking over her clitoris, sliding between her folds, her body writhing beneath him, her voice loud and clear, making his cock grow hard again. He'd longed to hear her freely moaning at his touch.

He slid one hand back down her leg, a finger along her pussy before slipping it inside her. Her back arched and she cried out as he thrust it inside her while his tongue circled her clitoris. She was getting close. One hand slid down her body, fingers curling in his hand, the other cupped her own breast, squeezing, pinching her nipple as she neared her climax. With a growl he licked her, his finger sliding in and out of her faster, faster, until she screamed, until her pussy gripped his finger, the muscles quivering around it with her orgasm. He pulled it from her, continuing to lap at her with his tongue, until her body stilled, her hand pushed at his head, and a whimper escaped her beautiful lips.

She lay on *his* bed, naked, her hair splayed out on the mattress, her cheeks pink, her eyes heavy with exhaustion, a soft smile on her lips, a satisfied smile. He never wanted to let her go and yet, that was exactly what he had to do. He lifted her, placing her head on the pillow, then crawled onto the mattress, pulling her back against him, his arm curled protectively around her, burying his face in her hair.

Could he have this, if he fought for it? Could he have her?

'You can't stay,' he said, a hint of sadness in his voice that he hadn't been able to conceal.

'I know,' she murmured. 'Maybe one day.'

His arm tightened around her as his heart squeezed painfully in his chest. Maybe one day. He was going to fight for her, for that one day. He wouldn't rest until she was his.

Chapter 18

Aladdin

Aladdin lounged in his room, propped up by more soft pillows than he had ever had in his life, made only of the finest fabrics. He lazily picked at the fruit platter that was placed in his room each day by servants who bowed to him. If his father could see him now, he would never be able to say Aladdin had no ambition.

The Djinn was watching him, his arms folded across his wide blue chest, an irritated scowl on his face. It was almost as if Aladdin's father was in the room. 'What is it, Djinn?' he asked impatiently.

'Are you not going to make your second wish?' he asked boredly.

Aladdin's eyes narrowed. 'Why are you so intent on me making my next wish?'

'I'm a Djinn, it's what I do,' the Djinn said vaguely, though Aladdin suspected there was more to the truth than that.

Aladdin had wondered what he might wish for to use his next wish. He had enough gold to do whatever he wanted. He could wish for a harem of beautiful women, and he'd spend many a night with them, with his pretty wife waiting for him, raising their children. He had many such musings but he couldn't think of a single thing he wanted that could not be fulfilled once he was sultan. It would be a waste to use his wishes for things that were already within his grasp.

'What would you wish for?' he asked, curious what an all-powerful being would want.

'That's easy. I'd wish to be free.'

'You can't just free yourself?' Aladdin asked.

The Djinn began to laugh. 'You truly are naïve. If I could free myself, would I be here with you?' he asked. 'Only my master can free me, and no master has ever wasted one of his wishes freeing a Djinn.'

'I might,' Aladdin said, watching as the Djinn raised his eyebrow. Aladdin shrugged. 'If I become sultan, what need will I have for wishes?' He grinned to himself at the very thought. When he was sultan, he wouldn't need a Djinn. He would have a whole palace full of staff scampering to attend his every whim. And it would be better, in that position, to free the Djinn so it couldn't be used against him.

'Now,' he said, casting a glance at the moon high in the sky. 'I have a princess to woo.' With a cocky grin, he strode from the room, pointedly ignoring the Djinn's disapproval. He'd managed to get her out of her clothes last time, this time, he hoped he might get something more.

He walked towards the princess's room with a lightness in his step that came from playing a winning game. He'd slipped past the guards so many times now that he could do it blindfolded. As he peered around the corner to check the coast was clear, he spotted Jasmine hurrying down the corridor, sneaking back to her room, a cloak bundled tightly around her, a warm blush on her cheeks, a soft smile on her lips, her hair tousled. It was a look he had imagined time and again, only in his fantasies *he* was the cause of it.

He couldn't sneak her out for a midnight rendezvous now.

She'd already had one with someone else. His teeth clenched in fury, his hands balling into white-knuckled fists as he marched back to his room, his mind whirling.

Aladdin slammed the door to his room, the sound echoing in the empty space. He knew one thing for certain, she'd been with a man. And it didn't take a genius to figure out who that man was. Who was the one who was so obviously displeased with his very presence, the one who always had his eyes on the princess, the one who had interrupted them at the lake with a look of pure fury that had, admittedly, scared the hell out of him?

Jafar.

What was he playing at? He couldn't marry her, he wasn't a prince. Was he content to ruin her? It was clearly something she was open to, but Aladdin needed her to marry him so he could become sultan. Everything hinged on his marriage to the princess.

Could he allow her to keep the advisor as a lover? No. He wouldn't give her up, he wouldn't share. He wanted the princess to look only at him, he wanted the most beautiful woman in the world for his wife, he wanted to be sultan, he wanted everything that came with it. He'd spent his whole life with nothing, and now everything was within his grasp. He wouldn't give that up.

'Back so soon?' the Djinn asked, inspecting his nails with a knowing smirk. 'The princess wasn't interested tonight?'

Aladdin ground his teeth but said nothing. He needed to remove Jafar from the picture, and he had the perfect means to do it. He had two wishes left. But he'd rather not waste a wish on the likes of Jafar if he could rid himself of the problem another way. Perhaps he could make the man see sense and back off. The sultan wouldn't take his word over Jafar's if he spoke up, and he had no doubt the princess would defend him.

The thought had him clenching his fists again.

'She didn't want to get naked with you after getting caught last time?' the Djinn persisted. Aladdin couldn't wait for the day he would be rid of the damned thing. But right now, he still needed it.

'In the lamp, Djinn,' Aladdin snapped, holding out the lamp.

'We had a deal. I get free reign if I got you out of the cave without a wish,' the Djinn said, a dark warning in his voice.

'Get in the lamp, I'm about to use my second wish,' Aladdin said.

The Djinn let out a frustrated sigh before doing as his master bid, disappearing into the lamp in a string of blue smoke. Aladdin secured the lamp to his belt, then checked himself in the mirror. He wanted to look the part if he was going to confront the man who dared to steal Princess Jasmine from him, the man who dared to ruin all his ambitions just when he'd discovered them.

It had taken Aladdin an annoying amount of time to find the Advisor's room. He'd never bothered to venture into that part of the palace before, he didn't have a need to. He'd expected to have the rest of his life to acquaint himself with the place, after all. But finally he found himself outside the fiend's door, banging on it with no restraint, his anger burning through his veins.

Jafar opened the door slowly, fully dressed in his dark robes, ugly sceptre in hand, nothing seeming out of place about him, which only fuelled Aladdin's anger. 'Prince *Ali*,' he sneered, a knowing smile toying on his lips. 'Or is it Aladdin?'

Aladdin stilled. The bastard knew. Another reason to get rid of him. The princess's little indiscretion may actually have helped him win the game, after all. Perhaps he would bring himself to forgive her, in time.

'Are you surprised?' Aladdin asked. 'When you kill someone, you should make sure he's dead.'

Jafar merely hiked a shoulder. Aladdin ground his teeth, his anger building in his chest. 'What brings you to my door?' Jafar asked, his tone bored.

'I know the princess was here,' Aladdin said, pulling out his trump card, a triumphant smile on his face. If Jafar had any sense, he would pause at that. It was the kind of information that could damn him.

'Yes, it seems she prefers my company to yours,' Jafar said smugly. 'And I don't think I'll give her to you.'

'Give her to me?' Aladdin roared, unable to hold his temper back any longer. He yanked the lamp from his hip and rubbed it until blue smoke filled the space, the Djinn appearing before them.

'You called, master,' the Djinn said, his tone bored, but interest shining brightly in his eyes.

'Djinn, I wish Princess Jasmine was in love with me,' Aladdin said. A triumphant smile spread across his face as

Jafar paled. It seemed he wasn't as unshakable as he made out to be.

The Djinn cleared his throat. 'You know I can't make anyone fall in love with you,' he said. Jafar's shoulders sagged in relief and Aladdin saw red.

He'd forgotten about those stupid rules. The Djinn couldn't kill anyone, either. His eyes widened in realisation. 'Then I wish for you to send Jafar to the end of the world.'

'Your wish is my command,' the Djinn said with a bow of his head.

'You should know, Jafar, I'm going to propose to her. She'll be mine before the week is out,' Aladdin sneered. Jafar opened his mouth as if to protest, but the Djinn clicked his fingers and his rival disappeared in a puff of blue smoke.

Aladdin grinned, then a chuckle burst forth. He'd done it. Jafar wouldn't be a problem anymore. Now Princess Jasmine would be his. He walked back to his room, a spring in his step. Soon he would marry the princess, become sultan, and free the Djinn before anyone could steal the lamp and use it against him.

But he wasn't stupid enough to free the Djinn yet. If he needed that last wish for any other complication, he would simply need to execute plan B and lock the useless thing up somewhere no one would ever find it again.

But for now, he had a proposal to plan.

Chapter 19

Jafar

When the smoke cleared, Jafar found himself on an island that was best described as a sandbar. The sound of water so loud it masked everything else as the ocean raced towards the edge of the world, falling into the universe like a massive waterfall. A watery mist danced lazily towards the sky, which was filled with more stars than he'd ever seen from Agrabah, as if this place were closer to the heavens than anywhere else on Earth. The stars set the ocean aglow with an ethereal light, making the scene before him both beautiful and terrifying. No man had ever been to the edge of the world and lived to tell about it.

That little bastard was going to pay for this.

He hadn't expected Aladdin would use a wish to remove him from the picture. He'd seen that look in men's eyes before, the look of a man with his eyes on a prize, and that prize was not Jasmine. She was a means to an end for him. He clenched his fist. That street rat didn't deserve her.

He meant what he said, he would *not* give her to Aladdin. And yet, she was the reason he was here. She'd made him lose his head. He'd chosen her over power, chose to spend his time with her instead of looking for a way to steal the lamp. He'd been playing the defensive when he should have been playing the offensive.

She was making him weak. But he didn't know if he could give her up.

He sat on the sandbar, staring out at the universe with frustration. He'd worked so hard to get to where he was, never letting anyone stand in his way. Now he'd let it all slip through his fingers because of a street rat and a princess that he could not seem to banish from his mind.

He'd never really made his move; too busy fighting his emotions, his desires, a fruitless struggle. Would she be his now if he'd only declared his intentions, his feelings for her? Would the sultan have accepted him?

But he didn't *want* to be the sultan, he'd never wanted to marry a princess, or anyone for that matter. Love makes you weak, love makes you do stupid things, illogical things. Love gets you beaten and left for dead in the street only to have your heart ripped out when you were too late.

And yet he couldn't decide what too late meant in this scenario. Was it losing himself in her only to have her taken from him by some illness, by childbirth, by an assassin? Or was it watching her slip through his fingers, watching her marry someone else?

He had never been stupid enough to covet something he couldn't have, his ambitions had always been reasonable, attainable. But she was neither reasonable nor attainable, she was fire and passion, she was stubbornness and determination, she was fair and good. So why had she given her heart to him?

He wasn't sure he deserved it. He wasn't sure he could give it back.

He wasn't sure it was his to keep.

He looked at his sceptre with a resigned sigh as a plan began to formulate. It wasn't like him to give up so easily, not when there was an answer so readily at hand. He had never used it for something so big before. The sceptre demanded a price for its power, and for something like this...he wasn't sure he'd survive.

But the alternative was to stay here on this sandbar and slowly die. The longer he waited the less likely he'd survive the spell. He couldn't wait to see the look on the street rat's face if he lived through this.

He took a deep breath, clearing his mind, focusing on his intention. He could feel the sceptre warming in his hand, the prickle of magic on his skin as it sparked through the air. He could feel the sceptre greedily accepting his offering, consuming his energy at an alarming rate. The world felt as if it was spinning and he kept his eyes closed, focused on his breathing, *concentrate*. When it finally stilled, his knees buckled beneath him and his stomach lurched. He forced his eyes open, looking up at the ceiling with blurred vision. He was so weak he couldn't call out, all he could do was lay there, wondering if he was going to die after all.

Darkness closed it, slowing eroding his vision as if taunting him, until he finally succumbed to it.

Jafar woke to a warm hand on his face, a drop of water splashing his cheek. His head resting somewhere soft and warm, but he couldn't open his eyes. A hand stroking his head gently, lovingly, the scent of jasmine on the air. She was the last person he wanted to see him like that. Anger stirred in his chest.

'Wake up, Jafar,' Jasmine pleaded, her voice shaky with tears. 'Don't you dare leave me. Not like this.'

That was all it took to dissolve his anger. His heart squeezed in his chest. He could feel his strength beginning to return. How long had he been out? Had the street rat already proposed to her? His eyes snapped open.

Jasmine's eyes widened as she gasped in surprise, the tears beginning to fall faster. 'So emotional today, princess,' he said with a cracked voice.

'I thought you were going to die,' she snapped, smacking him on the arm. He winced, surprised at how his entire body throbbed with pain. She gasped again. 'I'm sorry,' she said quickly, her lip quivering as she tried to hold back more tears.

'You shouldn't cry for a man like me,' he said, but he was secretly happy that she was. Happier than he should have been. He'd chosen her over power and it had led him here. On the brink of losing everything.

He would do it again in a heartbeat.

He looked at her hand, no ring adorned her finger. He let out a sigh. He still had time. But not much. He pushed himself to a seated position, her hands hovering around him as if she was waiting for him to fall. It should have irritated him, but instead it warmed his heart. It was a sign that she cared for him, a sign that she would accept him if he asked her.

The world spun and he blinked hard as it slowly righted itself.

'What happened to you?' she asked, looking at him with those sad eyes. He wished he could take that sadness away from her but he didn't know how. And he couldn't give her the answers she sought. Not yet.

'I'm alright,' he lied, though his strength was returning quickly now. His head stopped throbbing, the pain in his body dying down to a dull ache.

'That's all you're going to say? You were missing from court the entire day. I find you unconscious, and that's all you're going to say to me?' she asked, anger flashing in those beautiful eyes. It was better than seeing her sad.

'Yes, that's all I'm going to tell you. It's my problem and I will fix it.'

'Someone did this to you, didn't they? Who was it?' she demanded, her shoulders squared, the authority of a queen clinging to her.

'I told you I will fix it,' he snapped, rising to his feet. 'I don't need you to fight my battles for me, *princess.*'

That anger darkened her face as she rose to her feet. 'Try not to lose this time,' she sneered. She turned on her heels, marching from his room, swiping angrily at the tears on her face as she left him helplessly watching after her.

It was better for her not to know, in order for his plan to work, he needed to keep her in the dark. He only hoped she would forgive him for what he was about to do.

Jafar slept fitfully that night, but he still woke feeling like his old self. Rumour had travelled around the palace, Prince Ali planned to propose to the princess today. Excited chatter was in every inch of the palace as the staff and nobility all wondered if she would accept him. Jafar paced his room, grinding his teeth in frustration, knowing that many of them expected her to say yes, expected a royal wedding within the *month*.

She would no doubt expect him to stop it, to object to the union. He'd given her every reason to suspect his feelings were strong enough for such a public declaration. He could already see the disappointment on her face when he didn't show.

But the sultan had already given his blessing, had all but pledged her hand already. Would Jafar's interruption truly change anything?

Not to the sultan, perhaps, but he knew it would mean a lot to Jasmine. There was no doubt in his mind that she had given him her heart, she expected him to keep it safe but he was about to break it.

Prince Ali's proposal was the perfect time to steal the lamp. Iago would inform him as soon as the prince left his rooms, and then he would strike. Once the lamp was in his possession, Prince Ali would no longer be a threat. Jafar would expose him for the fraud he was, and he hoped Jasmine would come to forgive him, he hoped that she would come to understand that this was the logical move to make.

Though he knew that logic and emotion rarely went hand in hand.

He imagined her face when she realised he wasn't coming. Would she be hurt? Would those feelings she harboured for him turn to hate? Would she accept Ali in the heat of the moment?

Wait for me, Jasmine, he silently pleaded.

The door creaked opened and he stopped abruptly, turning to an out of breath Iago who nodded quickly. Jafar didn't wait another second. Maybe he could have everything, maybe he could get the lamp and still have time to keep that look from Jasmine's face. He raced through the corridors towards Aladdin's room. The palace seemed empty, no doubt everyone was trying to sneak a peek at the proposal, to see if they had won or lost their wagers. That suited him just fine.

He pushed against the door, finding it locked. He growled in frustration, holding his sceptre to the lock. It clicked, barely sapping any strength from him, and the door swung open lazily.

He sifted through drawers, cupboards, throwing the contents to the floor, his search becoming more frenzied with each minute that ticked by. The amount of silk and gold in the room was enough to make him sick. The street rat had so much power at his fingertips and he'd chosen to waste it on frivolities.

He slammed another door shut. Where the hell was it?! Each second he came up empty handed increased his anxiety. He could picture Ali down on one knee, the ring in his hand, he could picture her searching the crowd for him. He didn't want her to have to accept or refuse, he wanted to stop it, part of him wished he had simply done the foolhardy thing and stormed into that garden and declared his feelings.

But he didn't belong in the light, he operated best from the shadows. This was the logical thing to do, he reminded himself, this was how he would win.

He ransacked the bed next, chucking pillows out of the way, pulling back the blankets. Something glinted on the floor and Jafar rolled his eyes. Of course, it would be under the bed. He pulled the lamp out, a wicked grin spreading across his face. Finally, the lamp was in his possession and Aladdin was going to find out exactly who he had named as his enemy.

He tucked the lamp into his robes and hurried to the gardens where the proposal was taking place, hoping against all hope that he wasn't too late.

Chapter 20

Jasmine

J asmine sat at her mirror, her eyes puffy, an infuriating reminder of Jafar. Her heart had stopped when she'd seen him laying on the floor, his skin pale and cold. She thought he'd died. The flood of relief when she'd found a heartbeat had made her feel almost drunk, and tears began to spill down her cheeks. And instead of telling her what had happened or letting her comfort and care for him, he'd pushed her away.

Infuriating man.

Why did he always distance himself from her? She'd thought they had gotten past all that, she'd thought she'd convinced him to fight for her, for *them*. With a few words he'd put a chasm between them and she didn't know how she was supposed to cross it.

Was she fighting a losing battle?

Lina dabbed her skin with powder, each pat slowly hiding the signs of her distress. She would act as if he didn't exist. If he wanted to be alone, then she would let him. If he wanted forgiveness, he could come to her.

She stepped into one of her finest dresses, a beautiful blue that brought out her eyes. She let Lina place an intricate headdress on her, a bracelet on her wrist, rouge on her cheeks. Finally, her handmaid clicked her tongue.

'What?' Jasmine asked.

'Aren't you curious why I've dressed you like this?' Lina asked, her tone exasperated.

When Jasmine looked at herself in the mirror, she realised that it wasn't just the dress that was her finest. She looked as if she was going to attend a wedding. Her brow furrowed. 'I am now.'

'There are rumours that Prince Ali is going to propose to you today.'

Jasmine's stomach lurched. She did like Ali, but his wasn't the face she wanted to wake up next to every morning for the rest of her life. And yet, that man was not a prince, and even though she'd tried to incite him to fight for her, she feared she had failed. If she rejected Ali, what would happen? Would her father choose someone for her? At least she could be friends with Ali, even if she could never bring herself to love him.

And yet...

'There are worse choices, even if he isn't the man you love,' Lina said, a sad note to her voice.

'Lov – I don't...'

Lina tilted her head, raising that insulting eyebrow at her. Lina was right. She loved Jafar. But it seemed that her feelings were not returned. What did that mean? Those nights he'd touched her as if she was precious to him, was it all a lie? Was that how all men touched women, regardless of their feelings? Had she been blinded by her own emotions?

She let out a heavy sigh. 'It doesn't seem to matter.'

Lina threw her arms around Jasmine, squeezing her tight. Then she pulled back with a sniff. 'You go out there then and show him what he lost,' she said, her head high.

Jasmine forced a smile and squared her shoulders. She wanted to crawl into bed and cry. She wouldn't let him reduce her to that.

As she headed to the garden, a small part of her hoped that Jafar would come, that he'd stop the proposal, that he'd confess his love. Her father had always been fond of him. If he truly loved her, she was sure her father would allow it.

But as she entered the garden, which seemed busier than usual, his face seemed to be the only one missing.

The scene before her seemed perfect. The sun shone gently, the flowers burst with colour, the birds sang happily. Her father was smiling wide, looking genuinely happy for the first time since her mother's death, and her heart squeezed in her chest as she walked towards him.

Prince Ali looked confident, as if he knew exactly how the day was going to end. Each step she took made her feel heavier, as if she was being weighed down with stones. She forced herself to hold her head high.

Prince Ali finally noticed her arrival and he beamed up at her, that boyish charm shining through. She could feel the walls closing in around her as she stopped before him. She offered him a smile that didn't reach her eyes, though he hardly seemed to notice. Her father stepped aside, as if he was trying to give them space without drawing attention to himself.

How should a woman act when a proposal was coming? She couldn't seem to bring herself to be happy about it. 'You look beautiful, Princess,' Prince Ali said, and she noticed the lust in his eyes, though it was nothing to the intense desire she'd seen in Jafar's eyes when he looked at her.

Keep it together, she told herself as she felt tears pricking at her. 'Thank you. It's very busy in the garden today, almost as if the entire palace is expecting something.'

At her words several people turned away, pretending to be busy. Ali chuckled and ran a hand over the back of his head as if embarrassed, but she didn't believe it. Something felt wrong about it, fake. Was it because he wasn't who she wanted to be standing with now or was there something else behind her mistrust?

'That might be my fault. It's hard to keep a secret in a place like this,' he said.

'Especially if you don't want it to be a secret,' she said before she could stop herself.

He didn't seem to mind. 'You have obviously heard. I understand. You must be nervous, to be honest, I am a little, too.'

Her stomach lurched as she silently begged him not to say the words, wished for something, anything to stop what was about to happen.

'Since we first met, I have felt a connection with you. With our stations, it's rare to be able to marry with any kind of affection. Will you marry me and make me the happiest man on Earth?' he asked producing a brilliant diamond ring in a gold band.

She looked over at her father, tears were welling in his eyes, his hands clasped in front of him. She scanned the crowd, looking for Jafar, her heart cracking with each second she couldn't see him. Realisation hit then. He wasn't coming. He wasn't going to fight for her.

She turned back to Prince Ali, a tight smile on her face as she searched her mind for a response, but she couldn't seem to string a sentence together. Prince Ali slid the ring on her finger as if she'd said yes. Cheers went up around her, merging into a sea of white noise as she stared down at her finger, the foreign ring feeling wrong, cold against her skin as if she'd be shackled in iron.

'Stop!' a voice rang out and it made Jasmine stiffen. Jafar.

He marched down the stairs, a look of triumph on his face that made her heart sink. That wasn't the look of a man who'd come to fight for his love. He was holding a gold lamp in his hand and Prince Ali paled at the sight of it.

'Jafar,' Ali said, a nervous laugh escaping him. 'Have you come to congratulate us?' He took Jasmine's hand, holding it up as if he was showing off a prize. Her stomach lurched, anger stirring in her chest as she snatched her hand back.

'Jafar, what is the meaning of this?' the sultan demanded, his tone confused.

'Prince Ali is a fraud. He used this,' he said, holding up the lamp, 'to pass himself off as a prince.' He rubbed the lamp and blue smoke slipped from the spout, building into a big cloud. From that cloud emerged a man, tall and blue with a wide chest, but he seemed to be made of smoke from the waist down.

'What do you wish, master?' the Djinn asked Jafar.

Prince Ali seemed to panic beside her, his face pale, sweat beading on his brow. Jasmine looked at him, studying him closely. She'd asked him once which he was, a prince or a thief, and he'd lied to her face. She'd bought his lies, because she didn't care enough to look more closely at him.

Now she felt like a fool.

'Djinn, I wish for Aladdin to be what he truly is,' Jafar said, a wicked smile twisting his lips.

'As you wish, master,' the Djinn said. He clicked his finger and a puff of blue smoke surrounded Ali for a moment, dissipating to reveal Aladdin, dressed in the clothes she'd seen him in when they'd first met – old and worn with a thin coating of dust from the streets.

'You lied to me,' Jasmine said, her voice holding no emotion in it at all. She couldn't seem to muster any; no hurt, no surprise, no anger. Instead, her heart was aching for another reason.

'Yes. But Jasmine, listen,' Aladdin quickly said, a chorus of gasps around him as he used her name so brazenly. He ignored them and continued, 'I really did feel a connection with you that day. I never would have done this if not for Jafar. He used me to get the lamp and then he tried to kill me.'

'And you tried to kill me, so we're even,' Jafar growled. He clearly didn't believe they were even, and Jasmine knew he would kill Aladdin if he could.

She'd been such a fool. The entire exchange, Jafar had barely spared her a glance. Aladdin and Jafar, the whole time they'd been fighting a battle, fighting over something, but it hadn't been her. Not really. They'd been fighting over a magic lamp. Rage and humiliation twisted in her gut, searing at her like fire. She let out a laugh that sounded deranged. All eyes suddenly turned to her.

'Now I understand,' she said. She slid the ring from her finger, throwing it at Aladdin. 'You can keep that, you clearly need it more than I do.' She marched towards Jafar. 'And *you*,' she snapped, swiping the lamp from his hands, surprise clearly loosening his grip. 'You're despicable.'

She took a large step back, putting herself out of his reach. 'Princess, I –'

'Stop! I'll hear no more lies from *either* of you,' she seethed. 'The two of you fought so hard over the power of this lamp. It seems to me that *neither* of you deserve it. Djinn, I wish for you to be free.'

'No!' Aladdin and Jafar cried in unison. But it was too late. Smoke had engulfed the Djinn. When it cleared, her stood on the ground, with real legs. His skin was olive instead of blue, and he was shorter, more human in size. He patted his hands over his new body, his look of shock dissolving into one of pure joy.

At least someone can be happy today, she thought. She dropped the lamp and it clattered against the stone.

She marched past Jafar but he clasped her wrist, turning her to face him. She glared at him. 'I told you not to lose,' she said. She snatched her wrist from him and strode out of the garden, willing herself not to run as tears pricked at her eyes.

Chapter 21

Jasmine

'I told you not to lose,' Lina said as if she was reliving the best moment of her life. 'You are cold. I love it.'

'He deserved it,' Jasmine snapped, throwing her headdress on the bed angrily. She wasn't sure who she was most angry at, Aladdin for lying to her or Jafar for choosing a stupid lamp over her.

Well, that wasn't strictly true, but admitting it would make it hurt far worse than it already did.

'Yes, he definitely did. I'm so proud of you,' Lina said, sniffing and wiping away a fake tear. 'My little princess is all grown up.'

'This wasn't exactly a great day for me, Lina,' Jasmine grumbled. That was an understatement. It was hard to imagine how it could have been any worse. Jafar had shown up in the end, but he hadn't come for her. Her jaw clenched at the memory. She wished she could hurt him the way he'd hurt her, but in truth there really wasn't anything she could do to him. She resented that the most.

She'd done the one thing she could think of, she'd freed the Djinn and taken away their toy.

'I know, sweetie,' Lina said, wrapping an arm around her comfortingly. 'But in a way, it was a victory. You showed them that *you* are a queen not to be messed with. And now you don't have to marry Ali or Aladdin or whatever his name is. I hear he's in the dungeons right now. Maybe now you'll be free to marry whoever you want.'

Jasmine wondered how long he would remain in the dungeons. He would never be allowed free after what he pulled, unless she intervened. She wasn't entirely sure she wanted to, but part of her wanted him out of the palace so she didn't have to think about him again. If only there was such a simple solution to her Jafar problem.

'I don't want to marry anyone. Men are greedy liars who care about nothing but themselves and power.'

She'd longed so much for the love her parents had, the kind of love that would last a lifetime, even when one was gone and the other forced to stay behind. She'd thought she could have that with Jafar.

She'd thought wrong.

'Maybe one will surprise you one day. Perhaps he'll come and sweep you off your feet and make you forget all about Aladdin and Jafar. Until then, you can spend your evenings with me. We'll play cards and drink and gamble and do all the things we're not supposed to. Because. We. Can.' Lina grinned mischievously at her and she couldn't help but laugh.

With a friend like Lina, she could gladly swear off men forever.

A knock at the door interrupted them and they shared a look that said *who the hell is that?* As Lina strode towards it, Jasmine felt a spark of hope flickering in her chest that she begged to go away, but it persisted despite her request. She stared earnestly at the door, waiting with bated breath.

But the hope was misplaced, as her mind had said, even as her heart had refused to listen.

'Baba,' she said, quickly standing and inclining her head respectfully as her father entered the room slowly. His expression was uncertain, apologetic. He took her hands in his and smiled down at her. Pity. That's what she saw in his eyes. And she hated it.

'Jasmine, I'm so sorry. This is all my fault,' he said.

'Nonsense, Baba. Prince Ali fooled you as much as me,' she said, trying to comfort him. After all, it wasn't the prince who had upset her. She was relieved when it all came to light, when she realised she wouldn't have to marry him. But she couldn't tell her father that. Then she would have to explain everything and even if she thought he would understand, she just couldn't put herself through that. She wanted to put Jafar behind her and forget. Forget their time together, forget the things he'd said, the way he'd looked at her, forget the things he'd made her feel.

'I've been thinking, perhaps you were right. I was so wrapped up in keeping you safe that I didn't think about what was best for you and for our kingdom. So, tomorrow I will name you my heir. You will be sultan when I am gone and you will marry when you are ready.'

Tears pricked at her eyes, dripping to her cheeks. 'Baba!' she cried, throwing her arms around him, unable to help herself. He held her there for a moment before pulling away and clearing his throat, his ears tinged red. 'Well, good,' he said. He stroked her cheek once before nodding and leaving the room.

Lina's mouth hung open after she'd closed the door. 'Sultan!' she said excitedly and the two girls squealed together. For all the pain she had suffered, it seemed that something good was to come from the day after all.

'This calls for a celebration,' Lina said, hurrying to get two glasses out.

'Wine this time, Lina,' Jasmine said. She wasn't sure what would happen if her handmaid brought out the absinth again, but she had a very strong feeling it wouldn't be the sort of thing a sultan should be seen doing.

Jasmine stood outside the throne room wearing a beautiful white gown trimmed with gold. Lina had outdone herself, saying she needed to look the part, better than any prince, so she could show the room full of men that she deserved this honour.

She knew there would be many among them who disagreed with her appointment, but they would not argue with the sultan, especially after what they had witnessed in the garden.

The doors squeaked as they were opened and Jasmine took a deep breath. The throne room had been decorated elegantly with flowers and silks, a carpet of white led from the door all the way to the throne. It was as if her father was holding this ceremony like it was her wedding.

Married to a kingdom. It seemed more fitting to her than marrying a man.

She walked along the carpet, her step faltering slightly when she caught sight of Jafar, his black robes standing in stark contrast to the sea of white around her. There was something proud and sorrowful in his expression as he gazed at her, but she forced herself to look away, instead focusing on her father.

He had a proud expression as he watched her progression towards him. She bowed to him, sitting on her knees before him, touching her forehead to the floor in a show of absolute respect and loyalty.

When she sat back on her feet, the sultan gestured a hand and a man scurried forward. With a shaky hand he placed a crown on her head. 'Arise, my heir,' her father said. She did as he bid and the spectators began applauding, though she could sense the hesitation behind it. She may be the heir to the throne now, and she may one day be sultan, but she suspected that the battle was far from over. She would need to win the people's trust and their loyalty. As the first female sultan the kingdom would ever have, she knew the path ahead would not be an easy one.

But it was still better than marrying a man she didn't love so that he could rule in her stead. She would prove to them that she was a worthy leader.

A shriek burst through the crowd and Jasmine turned towards the sound. It felt as if time had slowed. She saw a man with his face covered by dark fabric so that only his cold eyes were visible. He was holding a knife, quite a small thing, really, shaped like an arrowhead. His eyes were locked on her and she had a thought; he was there to kill her. Was this how she would die?

The man drew his arm back, the guards ran toward him as the civilians scurried away in their fear, none brave enough to take on the assassin to save her. The man's eyes didn't waver, locked onto his target as he lined up his shot.

'Jasmine!' Jafar screamed her name, desperation and fear tangled in his voice.

She turned to him as the blade began to sail through the air, wanting his face to be the last thing she saw, even though he didn't deserve her love. She couldn't help but love him anyway. The blade pierced her flesh, embedding itself into her side, jutting between her ribs. She cried out as pain ripped through her, her body collapsing to the ground.

'No!'

Something warm trickled from her mouth, a scream sounded somewhere in the distance, heavy footsteps on stone, her eyes fluttered closed as her wound burned. She felt weak, she just needed to rest. If she could just rest for a moment, she would be okay.

'Jasmine. Jasmine, open your eyes. Stay awake,' a male voice said, thick with emotion as arms embraced her. The blade was pulled from her with a grunt that she distantly recognised as her own.

She forced her eyes open, Jafar's hovering over her, concern etched in his face, fear. Her heart ached. How could he look at her like that when he'd cast her aside for power? 'Why didn't you choose me?' she asked, her voice weak, shaky. She hardly recognised it. At her words his expression twisted, guilt, grief, sorrow. She closed her eyes, a single tear rolling down her cheek.

'No. Jasmine, stay awake,' Jafar begged, shaking her. But she didn't have the strength, she didn't have the heart, she let the darkness claim her.

Chapter 22

Jafar

Jafar paced the war room, his frustration reaching its peak as the old men stood around arguing amongst themselves, the embodiment of uselessness. Clacking like hens, each trying to impress the sultan with their brilliance, their strategic prowess. Every man present had attempted to take Jafar's job at one time or another. He saw them eyeing him, sizing him up as they bickered, wondering if he'd lost his mind, if he'd be weak enough now for them to seize power, even as their princess and future queen lay dying. The sultan was the only man sitting quietly at the head of the table, a grave expression on his face. He didn't seem to be hearing anything the hens were saying, not that they had noticed.

He'd never forget the look on Jasmine's face as she lay dying in his arms, the way she'd looked up at him as if he'd hurt her worse than any blade, and with her last words asked, *why didn't you choose me?* Her last words spoke of her heartache and it damn near ripped him apart. He wanted to take it all back, he wanted to forget Aladdin, he would storm that garden before the imposter could propose and claim her for his own.

She had been unconscious since her coronation. Days had passed and still she hadn't woken. The poison on the blade worked its way into her system, clawing at her, dragging her towards her end. The healers and physicians and gypsy witches had all been in, teams of them trying different methods. Anyone who had a claim to heal, whether they were scientific or mystic, was allowed an attempt, no doubt drawn by the reward that would come from success.

Please don't let those be her last words to me.

'Action must be taken. Arinia sent an assassin for the princess,' one of the advisors said angrily. Stating the obvious but not proposing a plan of action.

'Relations have been tense since the queen's death, we should instigate peace talks,' said another.

'If the princess wakes, perhaps we could arrange peace through marriage,' said yet another. Most of their bickering was like white noise, barely registering in Jafar's mind, but that *had* registered. He ground his teeth until he could take no more.

He stormed to the table, slamming his hands on the wood hard enough to stop their wagging tongues. 'Arinian attempted to assassinate the *crown* princess of our kingdom, the heir to the throne. You would reward that behaviour by *giving* them the kingdom?' he shouted, the old men flinching at his words. It was unthinkable that they would consider handing her over to her would be murderers. *If she wakes.* 'This cannot go unanswered. If it's war they seek, it's war we should give them,' he growled.

He was met with a long silence, stares from the hens as they assessed him with greedy eyes, still searching for a way to grab power. Finally, the old men began muttering amongst themselves, not daring to take their eyes from him, as if he were a mad man waving a sword around. Perhaps if he did wave around a sword they would stop muttering and prepare for war.

'Leave us,' the sultan said, keeping his eyes on Jafar. The old men fled the room with hurried bows, eager to get away from Jafar's wrath though that didn't stop their tongues from wagging in harsh whispers.

When they were alone, the sultan stood. Taking a deep breath, he looked over the map before him, running a hand over the dry paper, a grave expression on his face. Again he stared at that map as if it held all the answers he sought. Jafar had been so focused on his own emotions, he hadn't stopped to think about the sultan's. The man had lost his wife fifteen years ago to the Arinian's, and now he might lose his daughter. Jafar felt an unfamiliar emotion then: sympathy.

'Your majesty?' Jafar asked, trying to keep his tone neutral. Was he to lose his position because he couldn't keep his emotions in check? It was almost laughable how little it seemed to matter now. He'd give everything he had if only she would wake.

'I've seen that expression before. I know it well,' the sultan said, a hint of sadness to his voice.

'What –?'

'When you were holding my daughter, when you saw that she was dying, that you were losing her. It was the same look I had when I lost my wife,' he said, his eyes trained on Jafar. 'You love her.'

Jafar was silent for a moment. He'd worked so hard to keep his feelings to himself, and the one person who should never have found out was now confronting him with it. 'Your majesty, I'm sorry. I know it's wrong but I can't seem to help myself,' he said. He hated that he was standing before the sultan like a child to be scolded. He'd promised himself all those years ago that he would never be weak again, and yet, here he was, no energy left to lend to strength because it was all spent on thoughts of her.

'I'm not,' the sultan said. 'When Prince Ali proposed to her, she was searching the crowd. She was looking for you.'

She was looking for him? And what had he done? He'd come too late, come to take down his enemy rather than fight for her. *Why didn't you choose me?* Those words would haunt him for the rest of his life if she didn't pull through, if she couldn't be saved.

'If she wakes,' the sultan said, his eyes displaying a silent warning, 'don't disappoint her again.'

It took Jafar's brain a moment to catch up, to comprehend what the sultan was saying. 'Are you giving your blessing?' he asked, stunned.

The sultan gave one small nod before he ambled from the room, leaving Jafar alone with his thoughts once more. His treacherous thoughts. If he'd chosen her before it was too late, could he have had her? If she woke now, could he win her back?

He needed to see her.

The walk to her chambers was one he knew well now, having taken it several times a day since the attack. There were guards posted outside her door and at intervals down the corridor, their expressions grim but their eyes ever watchful. The sultan had put his best men on the detail, and though they were by far overqualified for simple guard duty, none of them begrudged it. They all understood the severity, the importance, of the task they had been given. They each nodded to him as he passed, pity in their eyes as if they had guessed the reason he visited her so frequently. There were probably rumours all around the palace, though he hadn't the time to keep up with the gossip of maids and old men.

He entered the room without a knock. He'd been told on his third visit to the room that he needn't bother. The handmaid always looked at him with such sadness, as if she knew more than anyone else. Had Jasmine confided in her?

'How is she?' he asked as the handmaid looked up at him. She looked tired, bags under her eyes, her skin pale, her hair rushed.

'Sometimes I think she's getting better, and sometimes I think I'm just hoping she's getting better,' she said with a sigh, placing a washcloth on the bedside table. She stood from the chair and indicated for him to sit, before shuffling into the bathroom. He could hear her muffled tears and it was like a stab in his chest, as if it was a sign that Jasmine really wasn't going to pull through.

He sat at her bedside and took her hand. Her forehead glistened with perspiration, her brows drawn in pain. He swallowed a lump in his throat and brought her hand to his lips, kissing it lightly before resting it against his cheek.

'It's time to wake up now, sweetheart,' he said softly, his voice cracking with emotion. 'Don't you dare go where I can't follow.'

Why didn't you choose me?

'You have to wake up so you can punish me for my stupidity,' he said, pushing a lock of hair from her forehead.

Once again he found himself at the sick bed of someone he loved, someone he couldn't save. He'd promised himself he wouldn't put himself in that position again, that if he did care for someone, this time he'd protect her. But he hadn't, had he? He'd tried to ignore his feelings instead, he'd chosen revenge over love, power over her. Power that she had then snatched away in the blink of an eye by setting the Djinn free. She could have wished for anything, but she hadn't cared about any of that.

He shouldn't have cared about any of that. She was so much stronger than him, in the end.

He didn't know how long he sat with her like that as she slept fitfully, her beautiful skin now so pale. As he looked at her, he felt as if he was watching her slowly slip away. In those first days he'd been unwilling to think that she wasn't going to make it, but now he feared that she really wouldn't wake from this.

He put her hand on the bed and stood, his joints feeling stiff. He pressed a kiss to her forehead, swallowing that lump in his throat again. 'Come back to me,' he whispered before finally dragging himself away.

Would he lose himself in work or drink tonight?

Chapter 23

Jasmine

Head pounding, throat dry like sand, body aching. She moaned, tried to move. Twitching her fingers. Someone gasped, hurried footsteps. Had someone said her name? She tried to open her eyes, they felt heavy. Her breathing laboured. She tried again, this time cracking them open. She winced against the light, her vision blurred. She blinked, then again, until her vision began to clear.

'She's awake. Send for the physician!' Lina called quickly. She looked down at Jasmine, stroking her hair, tears streaming down her face, her lip quivering. She picked up a glass of water and held it to Jasmine's cracked lips.

It took several moments for Jasmine to find the strength to speak, and Lina fussed over her the entire time. 'What happened?' she finally asked. She remembered the ceremony, the man with the knife. Remembered the pain as it pierced her body, the burning. She remembered Jafar's face as he held her, begging her to stay awake.

'You scared me half to death, that's what happened,' Lina said, her voice cracking as she wiped the tears from her face. 'You've been unconscious for a week. We'd started to lose hope. Lucky for us, the Djinn you freed knew how to cure the poison.'

'He did?'

'Yes, took him a long time to find the ingredients since he had to travel as a mortal,' Lina said.

Jasmine pushed herself up, leaning back against the headboard. The Djinn was in the room, a look of relief on his face, as if he'd also been worried she wouldn't make it. 'I owe you my thanks,' she said to him, trying to smile but her lips wouldn't cooperate.

'You owe me nothing, princess. You granted me my freedom when no other before you ever had. And you didn't even use a single wish for yourself. I would like to stay here and serve you,' he said.

'I'd be glad to have you, but I shall need a name to call you,' she said, then winced against a stab of pain. The throbbing in her head seemed to be dissipating, finally. She couldn't remember the last time she'd felt so weak. She was impatient to get out of the bed. She wanted a bath. Her stomach growled loudly. And some food.

Lina laughed happily and jumped from her seat to put some fruits on a plate. 'If I ever had a name, princess, I hardly know what it was anymore,' the Djinn said.

'How about Kareem?' she asked.

'You wish to name me generous and noble?'

She shrugged. 'You have spent a lifetime serving others, and when you were given the chance to do as you wished, you stayed to help me. To save me. I think the name is fitting.'

'I think it's a handsome name,' Lina said, taking her seat once more with a brilliant smile, her puffy eyes the only sign that she'd been crying. She brought a grape to Jasmine's lips.

'I can feed myself,' Jasmine complained, though she accepted the grape anyway.

'I don't care,' Lina said. 'I'm taking care of you. After the week I've had, you can just sit there and let me.' Tears began to well in her eyes again and Jasmine relented. She opened her mouth to accept the next piece of fruit.

Jasmine's thoughts went back to Jafar. It seemed even when she was on her deathbed, she couldn't put that man from her mind. Had he visited her over the past week? She wanted the answer to be yes, that would show that he did have feelings for her, even though he had chosen very wrong before, it would show he was redeemable. But she was afraid to ask. She was afraid the answer was no.

'You should be back to normal in a couple of days, so long as you rest,' Kareem said.

'Everyone is going to be so relieved – Oh, we should tell the sultan she's awake. And Jafar,' Lina said quickly, neglecting her feeding, her hand hovering out of reach with a piece of apricot.

'Why do you need to tell Jafar?' Jasmine asked, her brow furrowing.

'Don't be cross with him,' Lina said, her lip beginning to quiver again.

'Whyever not?' Jasmine asked, stunned to see what appeared to be sympathy in Lina's eyes. What had happened while she was unconscious?

The door opened, and she clicked her tongue. When had it become customary to just walk into her room without knocking? Jafar walked in, he looked tired, his cheeks shallower, as if he hadn't been eating, and her heart squeezed in her chest.

He stopped, as if frozen in place as he looked at her. He seemed lost for words and Lina's lip began to quiver harder, tears welling in her eyes. She put the tray of food down and she and Kareem slipped out of the room behind him.

'You're awake,' he said, sounding almost stunned. Lina told her not to be cross with him, but she couldn't help it, anger still nestled in her chest. He moved towards her as if he couldn't believe what he was seeing.

'So it would seem,' she said bitterly. Why was he looking at her like that? He'd chosen his little feud with Aladdin over her, why was he now looking at her as if he could finally breathe?

He sat on the edge of the bed, sweeping her into his arms, squeezing her tightly to him as if his life depended on it. 'God, I thought I'd lost you,' he said, his voice thick with emotion.

It was her turn to be speechless as she tried to make sense of her situation, wrapped in the arms of the man she loved, his scent enveloping her. She should resist him, she should make him grovel for her forgiveness, but in that moment she didn't have the strength to deny her feelings. She found her hands sliding around his back as she melted into him.

'Does that mean you forgive me?' he asked, his face buried in her hair.

'No.' She was aware that she sounded like a pouting child but she didn't care. She wasn't letting him off that easy, but right now, she needed this.

He chuckled as he kissed the top of her head. 'Well, I'll have to work on that.'

'Yes, you will,' she mumbled into his chest. She let out a contented sigh, feeling more relaxed that she had in a long time. He stroked her hair and she felt her eyes growing heavy, her senses beginning to fade slowly until she drifted into sleep.

As Kareem had said, Jasmine regained her strength with surprising speed. Jafar had visited her multiple times a day, which she had since learned from Lina he had been doing every day since her attempted assassination. She'd noticed an improvement in him, too. The colour returning to his face, the brightness returning to his eyes.

She was sure they would not be so bright if he knew what she was doing now.

She held the torch a little higher as she made her way down the cold, dark stairwell leading to the dungeons. She'd already spoken to her father, the letter for the guards clutched in her hands.

'Are you sure, Jasmine? After his treachery?' he'd asked.

'Yes, Baba. I'm sure. What he did was wrong, but I'm not hurt by his betrayal. I think maybe he did love me, in his own way,' she said. He'd been reluctant but he had accepted her request. She felt there was very little he would deny her now.

The guards scrambled to attention when she entered the dungeons. They'd been sitting around a table playing cards in the dim candlelight, by the looks of things. 'Princess,' they said, bowing respectfully.

'I'm here for the prisoner, Aladdin,' she said.

One of them pointed to a cell and she nodded her thanks. 'As you were,' she said with a smile. Maybe she would have some fun again after all this was behind her. She used to play cards with Lina and they would drink far too much. She was sure Lina cheated but she'd always ended up too drunk to remember to confront her. Maybe Jafar could remind her to do so in future. What a thought.

She approached the cell, lifting her torch higher so she could see in the darkness. Against the back wall, Aladdin sat shackled, a despondent look on his face. She felt a twinge of sympathy for him. At her approach, he looked up, his eyes widened.

'Princess?'

'Hello, Aladdin,' she said, offering a sad smile.

He moved towards the bars, his chains stopping him a meter before them. 'I'm sorry I lied to you,' he said, and she found herself believing him. 'When I saw you in that market place, I'd never seen anyone so beautiful. I only wanted...' he trailed off shaking his head. 'It all went so wrong.'

She offered him a smile, somehow feeling guilty. She supposed she had led him on, her sneaking out had led them to this point. But she also suspected that the power within his reach had corrupted the easy freedom she'd once seen in him, twisting him with ambitions beyond his grasp.

'I've come to offer you your freedom,' she said, holding up the letter in her hand. 'My father has signed it.'

His mouth fell open and he shut it again. 'Why would you do that?'

She shrugged. 'I was feeling merciful. I also felt bad that you were locked up in here when I wouldn't have married you, anyway.'

'But...' he said, seeming surprised, but he trailed off, then nodded. 'Jafar.'

That guilt returning to her. Though she was sorry for how the situation had played out, she wasn't sorry for her feelings towards Jafar. 'Yes. I love him.'

'I never stood a chance, did I?' he asked, his expression resembling that of the carefree boy she'd once met on the streets of Agrabah. Perhaps his feelings for her hadn't been as deep as he'd imagined them.

'Since I've had my chance to find love, I want to give you a chance, too. Maybe when you find her, you'll do better.'

'Perhaps. Although I think I'm sworn off love, at least for now. Maybe my father was right, after all. Maybe I need to do something more with my life.'

'Now would be as good a time as any, what better time for a fresh start?' she asked, her feelings of guilt beginning to lessen.

'And how does Jafar feel about my release?' Aladdin asked.

'He doesn't know yet, so if I were you, I wouldn't stay here too long,' she said with a teasing smile. 'Goodbye, Aladdin.'

She handed the letter to the guard before walking back up the stairwell, feeling like a weight had been lifted from her shoulders.

Chapter 24

Jafar

J afar headed for Jasmine's room, nerves slithering in his stomach. Of all the places he'd seen himself when he'd imagined his future, this was not one of them. And yet it felt like the most important thing he would ever do.

Jasmine had improved dramatically over the last few days, the colour returning to her cheeks, the strength returning to her body, until she finally seemed fully recovered, much to the relief of the entire kingdom. But today he hadn't seen her. He'd been busy with affairs of state, the sultan insisting that he be present. He couldn't help feeling that he was being punished for something, which was a ridiculous thought. When had he been the kind of man to be so obsessed with a woman?

Since the day Jasmine had returned home, he realised.

He knocked on the door, something that still took active thought after a week of just walking in, but he had walked in on her dressing once and she'd yelled at him, 'You can't just walk in here as if I were your wife!'

Not yet, he'd thought.

'Come in!' Lina called out.

'What? Are you crazy?' Jasmine protested, just as the door opened.

His mouth nearly dropped at the sight of her, sitting at her mirror with her hair loose, wearing a nightdress that reminded him of the night she'd snuck into his room. She frowned at him in the mirror, though she made no moves to cover herself.

'It's not fair if you two are in cahoots to work against me,' she grumbled.

Lina merely laughed merrily as she fled the room, knowing full well what was to come, else she wouldn't have dressed Jasmine like that. He'd sworn her to secrecy, although he was surprised she'd managed to keep it. She had been so excited when he'd told her, anyone would have thought she was the heroine of the tale. But he'd needed her help.

When they were alone, Jasmine let out a sigh before rising to her feet, a movement that drew his eyes to her figure. She acted put out, but he noticed desire had begun dancing in her eyes.

She closed the distance between them with sensual steps. She stopped too far away, just out of reach, a silent challenge. A challenge he wanted to accept, but he had something he needed to do first. Something he didn't even know how to start. When he didn't move, she tilted her head, no doubt searching his face for the reason, perhaps wondering what game they were playing tonight.

'What brings you to my room so late in the evening, Jafar?' Her voice was sultry, seductive, making him want to rip her dress from her and cover every inch of her body with his lips.

Not yet.

'You're not a very patient princess, are you?' he asked. It wasn't like him to be nervous. He mentally shook himself and reached into his pocket. 'I came to ask you something.'

He pulled the ring out and presented it to her, and her eyes widened in complete surprise. He knew she'd already guessed what he was going to ask her, she was too bright for her own good, but the ring in his hand was special. A ruby in the centre of a gold band, three small diamonds on either side. It wasn't the grandest ring, or even the most expensive. But rubies had been her mother's favourite.

'My mother's ring?' she asked, tears welling in her eyes. 'Then Baba has given his blessing?'

The look in her eyes was so beautiful his heart nearly stopped. She looked at him as if he hung the moon, as if he was her everything. No one had ever looked at him that way before. 'He has.' She ran to him then, flinging her arms around him. He could feel her tears soaking into his robes.

'I haven't asked you yet,' he said.

'It doesn't matter. My answer is yes,' she said, her voice muffled by his shoulder.

He couldn't help smiling and he wrapped his arms around her. He almost couldn't believe it was happening. His whole life had been about collecting power, about protecting himself. He realised now that he hadn't truly been living, trapped in a goal to survive, a goal that was left over from a time when he'd had no control. And he'd almost let the best thing in his life slip by him. 'Does this mean you forgive me now?'

'Maybe.'

'It seems I still have some convincing to do,' he said, prying her from him to slip the ring on her finger. He looked into her eyes, her hand still clasped in his. 'Now, you are mine.' He captured her lips in a searing kiss, his arm snaking around her waist to pull her tightly against him. She gasped, and he took advantage of her parted lips, sliding his tongue between them to deepen the kiss. Her hands gripped his robes, fingers curling into the fabric as she pushed herself to her toes to get closer, her breasts pressing against his chest. He was growing hard, could she feel it? If she could, it did nothing to quell her passion as she licked at his tongue, moaning against his lips.

A need grew in him like he had never known before, as if the ring on her finger had opened a floodgate. Nothing stood between them now except what was considered proper, and none of it would matter after the ceremony. He couldn't wait any longer, he had to have her.

He pulled back, their shallow breaths mingling in the silent room. He slipped behind her and began unbuttoning her dress, slowly, his finger grazing her skin with each one, loving the way her body shuddered at his touch. He dropped his lips to her neck as he popped the next button open, letting his breath caress her skin. Goosebumps raced across her body and she moaned, melting into him.

He slid the sleeves down her arms, hands gliding against her skin as he kissed her nape, slowly moving across to her shoulder. He pushed the dress down, hands trailing down her sides, her ribs, her waist, sliding the fabric over her hips. It rustled as it fluttered to the floor, forgotten.

His hands continued exploring her body, sliding over her stomach, up to cup her breasts, her head falling back against him as she sighed contentedly. His thumbs brushed across her swollen nipples and she moaned, more of her weight on him as her body softened under his touch, her eyes fluttering closed. With one hand still palming her breast, the other slid back down her stomach towards her panties. She rolled her hips, awaiting his touch. He slipped beneath the fabric, his fingers sliding between her folds to rub slowly against her clitoris.

'Already wet for me,' he murmured, desire leaking into his voice.

He needed *more*.

He released her, taking his own clothes off and tossing them to the floor. She was already raking her gaze over his body with a hungry look in her eyes that sent a shudder of anticipation through him, his cock stiffening under her gaze as it settled there, her tongue darting across her lip.

He wanted those lips wrapped around his cock, but he wanted to be inside her more. *Needed* it. He pulled her to him roughly, lifting her quickly. She wrapped her legs around him, the head of his erection brushing against her core and she moaned as she pressed her lips to his. Her arms snaked around his neck, fingers curling in his hair. He wondered what it would be like to press her back against the wall and take her, but he filed that fantasy away for later. This was her first time, he would need to be gentle, patient, though he had been waiting so long for this he wasn't sure he had it in him. He carried her to the bed, laying her down on the blanket. He long dark hair fanned out around her, her swollen lips and nipples calling to him, begging for his kiss.

He hovered over her, his lips trailing down her neck, slowly over her collar bone, down her chest. Her back arch as he neared her breasts, and he latched onto one, flicking his tongue over it as he sucked. Her eyes fluttered closed as she gasped, her hands fisting the sheets beneath her. As he released it, she whimpered, but he didn't give her what she wanted, his eyes on a bigger prize. His lips trailed down her stomach, his hands running over the contours of her body. He kissed the sensitive skin above her panties, his fingers sliding inside the fabric as he began easing it down her legs, his lips stopping just short of her centre. He could see how wet she was for him as he continued sliding the fabric down, over her shins, her feet, finally flinging them to the floor as if he never wanted to see them again. Which he didn't. If he had it his way, she'd never wear panties again.

He positioned himself between her legs, pushing them wider to give him better access to her. She shivered in anticipation as his breath caressed her flesh, his arms slid under her legs, hands gripping her hips. A wicked smile curled his lips as he blew gently onto her wet opening, and she gasped, writhing in his grip, her hips rolling up, desperate for the touch he denied her.

'Tell me what you want, love,' he murmured, then began to gently blow again.

'Are you going to make your queen beg?' she asked, her voice breathy, her body trembling with need.

He smirked then. 'Oh yes,' he said, mostly bravado. If she refused to, he doubted he could hold himself back much longer. 'Beg for me, my queen.'

Her hands twisted in the sheets, pulling them tighter, her hips rising for his tongue, her teeth sinking into her lip to keep her from relenting. She was a stubborn queen. He flicked his tongue over her clitoris, the lightest of touches, and she whimpered. *'Beg for me,'* he growled. He sank his teeth into her inner thigh, as much to stop himself from relenting as to coax her into it. She gasped, body writhing as he sucked at her, leaving his mark on her skin.

'Please, Jafar,' she begged.

His tongue was on her before she finished, licking between her folds, flicking over her clitoris as she writhed, her voice filling the room. Her fingers tangled in his hair, holding him close, needing more. He dug his fingers into her hips, pulling her firmly against his tongue and she moaned. Her hips bucked and he knew she was already close. His cock pulsed. He was one step closer to being inside her. He fervently licked at her, mercilessly stroking her with his tongue, her grip tightening on him. She was so close, he could taste it. He growled against her, the vibration sending her over the edge as she thrashed on the pillow, her cry echoing in the room. He continued to lap at her, his erection painfully hard, eager to be inside her. She began to push against him feebly, as if all the strength had been drained from her. When she whimpered, he finally relented.

She lay back against the mattress, her hair wild around her, lust colouring her cheeks, her eyes heavy. 'We're far from done, love,' he murmured, his voice husky with desire.

Her teeth toyed with her bottom lip, a spark in her eyes letting him know she was ready for more. His cock pulsed, the head growing slick with anticipation. He pushed her legs apart as he knelt between them, he gripped his cock and began sliding it over her slick pussy. She gasped, arching her back, her taut nipples grazing his chest. Her teeth sank into her lip as she moaned.

'Tell me what you need, my queen,' he said as she rolled her hips up to him. He could feel her warm entrance against his cock, the temptation almost killing him.

'I need you inside me,' she said, her voice so deliciously wanton.

He swallowed hard, hoping he had the strength to be gentle with her. He had prepared her as best he could. He pressed against her opening, the head of his cock slipping inside her and she moaned. He slowly inched his way inside her, watching her closely. Each time she stiffened, he would pause, letting her get used to him, waiting for her to relax before feeding her a little more. When he was finally buried deep inside her, perspiration had begun to form on his brow, his arms shook with the effort to control himself.

'Alright, love?' he asked.

She nodded up at him and he leaned down to kiss her gently. She greedily kissed him back, her muscles clenching around his cock with need. The last of his control crumbled. He slid back and thrust into her, and a cry of surprised pleasure fell from her lips, her hands climbed his body as he bucked his hips against her, nails digging into his back, legs wrapping around him. Her eyes fluttered closed as she lost herself in the pleasure. He could feel the pressure building in his cock, knew he wouldn't last much longer. With a final thrust, she arched her back, crying out as her orgasm rocked through her. Her muscles clenching around him, milking the orgasm from him with a guttural growl.

They lay there for a moment, still completely connected, chests heaving with every panting breath. Finally, he rolled on to his side, gazing down at her. The blush to her cheeks was almost bashful now, as if she couldn't believe what she had just done. He pushed a stray strand of hair from her face and she gazed back at him, the pure love he saw in her eyes robbing him of breath. He began to feel a blush of embarrassment rising to his own cheeks, so he turned her around, tucking her to his side as he absently stroked her skin. He wished he could stay with her, but it would be scandalous if anyone found out what they'd just done. But he could at least stay with her until she fell asleep.

Though there was no way he was going to be able to stay away from her for even a single night now. The sooner they were married, the sooner he could trap her in their bed for days, the sooner he could keep her through the night and wake up to her every morning.

He would never have thought it possible, but he had never wanted anything so badly in all his life.

As her breaths began to steady, growing deep with sleep, he kissed her temple, reluctantly releasing his hold on her. 'Good night, my love,' he whispered softly before forcing himself to leave her side, knowing that soon he would never have to do so ever again.

Epilogue

Lina sniffed with teary eyes as she gazed at Jasmine, a mixture of satisfaction and joy in her face. Jasmine would never expect anything less, Lina wasn't afraid to be proud of her work, and she had done a splendid job this time. Jasmine had never been so beautiful in all her life, and as she took in the swaths of white silk, the shining gems that adorned her dress, the henna on her hands and feet, she couldn't help wondering what Jafar would think when he saw her.

'I can't believe you're going to be married,' Lina said.

'I can hardly believe it myself,' she admitted.

A month ago, Jafar had proposed to her with her mother's ring. She'd been so surprised because that ring had shown her that her father approved the match, that he had already consented to their being married, something she had scarcely dared to hope for.

She'd wanted to get married right away, but there was a process that had to be followed, and she couldn't bring herself to deny her father in this. His only daughter was getting married, and he'd allowed her to marry the man she loved, so she forced herself to be patient.

In that time, Jafar and her father had worked tirelessly securing the kingdom's safety with treaties and allies. Her father's way. She was secretly glad they weren't going to war, she didn't want to lose her husband before he even claimed the title. Instead, they'd built strong alliances, all of whom were more than happy to end trade agreements with Arinia should they make any attempts on Agrabah again.

Meanwhile, wedding preparations had begun. Invitations sent out to every kingdom, except Arinia, and more people attending than she knew what to do with. The preparations didn't bother her, she was hardly allowed to do anything for them. Teams of staff were taking care of everything, and a very intense woman was running the entire show. Jasmine made a point of avoiding her wherever possible.

It was hard to believe that the day had finally arrived. No more sneaking around. Since that first night, Jafar had spent a lot of time in her room in the evenings, and if he was busy with work, which happened more often than she'd like, she would sneak into his room to pry him away from it.

'Are you ready?' Lina asked.

Jasmine took a deep breath, gave herself a last look in the mirror, then smiled wide. 'I've never been so ready for anything in my life,' she said, excitement dancing with nervousness in her stomach. This was it.

Lina led her from the room towards the garden where the ceremony was being held. She could hear the quiet buzz of hushed conversations, the fluttering of insects. The sun beamed down with a gentle touch, lighting up the vibrant flowers, enticing the birds to song. A gentle melody was being played on a lute as the crowd waited for her arrival.

At the head of it all, standing at the end of a white silk carpet, was Jafar. For the first time in her life, she saw him standing there in white, gold trimming his sleeves, his seams. His dark hair spilled down his neck, his hands clasped together in front of him. He looked nervous. It was the first time she'd ever seen the emotion on him and it made her smile as she stepped into the sun, her bare feet touching the silk.

She was finally going to marry the man she loved.

Jafar's eyes widened as Jasmin stepped onto the aisle. The sunlight illuminated her, shining off the tiny jewels on her dress, drawing every eye to her. But what drew him in most was that smile on her face, that perfectly contented smile, soft and gentle. She truly was the most beautiful creature he had ever beheld, and soon she would be his.

As she made her way towards him, her bare feet slipped out from beneath her dress, henna painted on her skin in intricate patterns of gold and brown. All eyes were on her, but her eyes never strayed from him. It made his heart thump against his chest. If this was a dream, he never wanted to wake.

When she neared, he held out his hand for her, and she placed her delicately painted one in it without hesitation, her smile widening, excitement dancing in her eyes. All he could think was that he couldn't wait for the ceremony to be over so he could rip her out of that dress. For the first time, he wouldn't have to sneak out before anyone could see.

They turned to the minister, standing proudly at the head of the ceremony, no doubt feeling a great deal of importance at being the man to preside over the royal wedding. He nodded his head and a young man began chanting, the words lilting around them as he tied their joined hands with a strip of white silk. They raised their hands, stepping slowly around the ceremonial fire, the heat of the flames rising up to greet their skin as they circled it, his eyes never leaving hers.

He remembered practicing the ceremony. It was so old fashioned to him. Weddings where he grew up were much simpler, probably because there was so much less money to be spent. He'd been told the steps around the fire were symbolic of a couple choosing to face the hardships of life together, to remain strong and united against any foe or tragedy. It was beautiful, he supposed, but he didn't need a symbolic gesture to know he would always be by Jasmine's side no matter what befell them.

The chanting ceased and they resumed their positions, side by side. The minister offered up a prayer, his eyes skyward. When he finally looked back at them, Jafar turned to face Jasmine, a nervous fluttering in his stomach. He'd never been one to enjoy attention, he preferred to work from the shadows, going unnoticed. But now all eyes were trained on him, and they forever would be from this day forth.

'Jasmine, I take you as my wife. I take you as you are. Loving everything that I know of you, trusting what I have yet to discover, I vow to respect and trust you, as long as we both shall live,' he said. He'd practiced the words so many times but they had never felt more real than in that moment, saying them to her as if the entire world had fallen away.

She looked back at him with teary eyes and he could tell by the stubborn set of her jaw that she was trying not to cry. He had never loved her more than he did in that moment. He knew that she would be an incredible queen, and where she longed to show the world what she was capable of, he knew that his place was by her side, supporting her from the shadows. He'd never wanted to rule, but she did. She was born for it. It was another way in which they were perfectly matched, another sign that they were two sides of the same coin.

She took a breath to steady herself. 'Jafar, I take you as my husband. I take you as you are. Loving your faults and your strengths, as I offer myself to you with my faults and my strengths. I vow to respect and trust you, as long as we both shall live.'

The minister sniffed. 'You may kiss the bride,' he choked through tears as the silk tie was removed.

Jafar pulled her to him, capturing her lips in a searing kiss, salted from her tears. For the first time in his life, he felt pure and unadulterated happiness, the kind of joy he had always thought to be a myth.

For the first time in his life, he looked forward to the future, he looked forward to *living*.

What did you think of The Magic of the Lamp?

Thank you for reading The Magic of the Lamp.

If you enjoyed the book, please take a moment to post a review on Amazon or Goodreads. Your feedback and support will help me improve my writing craft for future projects (and inspire me to keep writing!)

Stay in the loop! Subscribe to my mailing list to get all the news straight to your inbox, as well as access to a free ebook and bonus content!

www.loreleijohnson.com/subscribe

Thank you for your support and happy reading!

About The Author

Lorelei Johnson is an Australian author who writes tantalising romances that will leave you wanting more.

While Lorelei typically writes paranormal romance, she will sometimes stray from that path to venture into the unexpected.

In her collection you'll find a variety of seductive romances featuring swoon-worthy men and feisty women. You're bound to find the HEA you're looking for.

Books by Lorelei Johnson

The Tantalising Tales Collection

My Sweet Cinderella
Scarlett and the Wolf
Beauty and the Beast
The Touch of Snow
The Little Mermaid
Summoned by the Piper
Rumpelstiltskin
The Magic of the Lamp

Loved by the Zodiac

Loved by Aries
Embraced by Scorpio
Claimed by Leo
Cherished by Taurus
Treasured by Virgo

Manufactured by Amazon.com.au
Sydney, New South Wales, Australia

11478179R00118